A
MUMMY
TO DIE FOR
The Coffee House Sleuths

A MUMMY TO DIE FOR

TO DIE FOR

The Coffee House Sleuths

T. LOCKHAVEN

EDITED BY:
EMMY ELLIS
DAVID ARETHA
GRACE LOCKHAVEN

TWISTED KEY
publishing

2020

First Printing: 2020

ISBN 978-1-947744-61-5

Twisted Key Publishing, LLC
www.twistedkeypublishing.com

Ordering Information:
Special discounts are available on quantity purchases by corporations, associations, educators, and others. For details, contact the publisher at the above listed address.

U.S. trade bookstores and wholesalers: Please contact Twisted Key Publishing, LLC by email twistedkeypublishing@gmail.com.

Contents

A
MUMMY
TO DIE FOR

Chapter 1

Hunted

Something was there, lurking in the shadows, hidden behind rich green leaves and thick stalks of towering bamboo. In the darkness, two glowing orbs stared hungrily. It was a jaguar, peering out at its prey, ready to pounce.

This dramatic scene described the shirt Michael West wore that bright sunny morning.

He felt like a muscular, sinewy jungle cat as he strode into the Bitter Sweet Café in his newly tailored, athletic-fit shirt. Every eye was on him as he approached the counter, and rightfully so. An apex predator had just entered, and he was on the prowl.

"Michael," a high-pitched voice called out.

Here it is—the ladies can't resist a well-dressed man steeped in mystery and dripping with intrigue.

"Yes," Michael said coolly, swiveling his head toward his first admirer, cocking an eyebrow.

"Your fly's open." Mary Taylor, a petite eighty-year-old woman, jabbed an arthritic finger at

Michael's shorts, just in case he was unsure of the location.

Michael's face grew hot. Instead of admiration, he'd been felled by a feisty woman in a matted blonde wig. He hunched over and tucked a small errant triangle of his shirt back into his fly and zipped his pants.

"That's better," Mary nodded. "Young folks these days, not a modicum of decency." She turned her attention back to her cup of coffee, the rim covered in smudges of hot-pink lipstick.

"I have to remind my grandchildren every time they go to the bathroom," Hellen Morris whispered loudly to the women at her table.

Her tablemates bobbed their heads knowingly.

Michael glanced down, smoothed the front of his shorts with his hands, and then gave a curt nod to Mary, who shooed him away with her hand. A series of snickers and a lone catcall filled the café.

Michael made his way to the front counter. His swagger decimated by a woman his mother's age, he looked for some comfort from his friend Ellie, co-owner of the Bitter Sweet Café.

Ellie was bent at the waist sliding a fresh pan of buttery croissants into the glass display case. She stood and brushed her brown ponytail from her shoulder.

"I saw your entrance." Her brown eyes sparkled mischievously. She brushed some baking powder from her cheek and poked Michael in the chest with a spatula. "I think everyone in here had the same thought when they saw your shirt."

"Who is that majestic creature, blessing us with his presence?"

"Not quite." Ellie placed her hands on her hips. "Really, Michael. That shirt looks like those garish, felt, Elvis black light posters that street vendors used to sell."

"Funny you should mention that. If you turn the lights off it glows. All you can see are the eyes of the jaguar."

"Let me guess, you tried it."

"In the closet, as soon as it arrived," Michael boasted.

"Dear Lord, Michael...," Ellie sighed. "Do you ever think about what you're about to say? No wonder the kids beat you up at school."

"Admit it, Miss Banks, you find me adorable." Michael smiled.

"More like deplorable. And get your sweaty elbows off my counter."

"My elbows don't sweat, they glisten."

A timer went off behind Ellie, and she scurried away from the counter, grabbed an oven mitt, and pulled the door open. She slid out a tray filled with golden-brown cupcakes.

"Those smell great," Michael said, sniffing the air.

"Family recipe. They're for Arthur's birthday." Ellie nodded toward an old prickly man in a pointed birthday hat and a T-shirt that read "Birthday Boy."

"Good ole Arthur. How old is he?"

"Eighty-nine."

"Wow, good for him. You know what?" Michael whispered conspiratorially. "His T-shirt should say 'Birthday Fossil.'"

Speaking of fossils, Michael's tone became suddenly serious. "Have you seen the picture of the human footprint taken beside the dinosaur track in Texas?"

"Of course, it's a famous picture."

"That was Arthur's footprint, in that picture."

Ellie sighed loudly. "Sorry to burst your bubble, buddy, but that story was debunked in the late '80s."

"Are you sure?" Michael asked.

"Quite." Ellie nodded and wiped off the countertop where Michael had rested his elbows.

"Well, that's disappointing," Michael sighed.

Michael took a sip of his coffee and casually gazed out over the café. He wondered what he'd be like when he reached Arthur's age—if he reached his age. The words "Happy Birthday" were attached to the wall above Arthur's head. Below hung a series of pictures, a history of his life. One of the pictures showed Arthur in his thirties, wearing a leather pair of goggles. He'd been a promising race car driver. But in a freak wreck in Charlotte, he'd killed not only his teammate but his best friend. He left racing, carrying the weight of his friend's death on his shoulders, and joined the Marines. After nineteen years in the military, he retired, and at the age of fifty-four, he moved back to Lana Cove.

The next pictures touched Michael's heart. Ellie had told Michael that when Arthur returned, the guilt of his friend's death began weighing him down again. His friend's family still lived here, and he felt he'd never be able to face them again. However, the people of Lana Cove reached out to him, surrounding him with love and kindness. There were a half a dozen photos of Arthur with his friends.

One picture taken about twenty years ago showed Mary Taylor and another woman Michael didn't recognize kissing him on each cheek, like an Arthur sandwich. His smile stretched from the corners of his lips to his eyes. Now, at the age of eighty-nine, Arthur was surrounded by friends who truly loved him. Yes, he was grouchy and irritable, but Arthur was indeed a good man.

Michael had fled from his own pain and sorrow and found himself here in Lana Cove, a quaint seaside town, just past the Virginia state line. Yeah, the locals were quirky, but then again, so was he, and that's why he felt like he fit in here. He'd been in a loveless marriage and been trapped in a thankless job that slowly consumed him like a cancer, creeping along, taking his very existence from him.

He hadn't realized how bad it had gotten until he was standing in the airport terminal, a forty-year-old man, kissing his daughter goodbye as she left for college. The little girl, now a woman, walking away, pursuing her own life, her own dreams. Instead of being a father, he'd worked through his daughter's middle school and high school years. He'd reasoned that his absence from her life was a necessary sacrifice so she could attend the best private schools and get into the college of her choice. *Did I make the right decision?* A sharp pain lanced his heart. *I miss her.*

Chapter 2

Arch-Nemesis

A soft melodic jingle snapped Michael out of his thoughts. He glanced toward the front door and gasped. A manly figure filled the doorway, golden sunlight radiating around him. He looked like a Greek god.

The man removed his sunglasses and slipped them in his shirt pocket. He ran his fingers through his mischievous, dirty-blond hair as his hazel eyes narrowed, adjusting to the light in the café.

Arthur Wisely stopped gesticulating, Ellie stopped wiping down the counter, and Michael stopped breathing. *Who is this man?*

Then, without warning, the man smiled. A few feet behind him, Mary Taylor gasped, and then came the clanging sound of a piece of silverware striking the floor.

A young, beautiful woman with hair the color of honey, golden-colored skin, brown eyes as moist as homemade brownies, a petite nose, and plump lips that would make any Botox sales rep jealous stepped into the doorway beside him, interlacing her arm in his.

As a pair, they walked to the front counter. The man turned his attention to Ellie and gave her a dose of his dazzling smile.

"Ah, good morning." His voice was smooth, elegant. "Are you the owner of this gorgeous establishment?" His eyes glistened as he addressed Ellie.

"British," moaned Michael. *Of course, he had to have a British accent.*

"Yes, I'm Ellie Banks." She brushed a few flyaways from her forehead and smiled back at the man. "Do I know you?"

"Ellie, Ellie, Ellie, what a beautiful name." He moved his head from side to side as if savoring it. "Shining light."

"Pardon?" Ellie asked, confused.

"Your name. In Greek, it means shining light, and in Hebrew, its origin language, it means God is my light." He studied her face for a moment. "And I see that you were named appropriately."

Ellie narrowed her eyes and smiled uncomfortably, not sure how to respond to such unexpected attention. "Uhm, thank you."

"Forgive me," he exclaimed. "I'm being incredibly rude. My name is Hugo. And this is Whitney, my partner in crime."

"Nice to meet you, Ellie." The woman's voice reeked of disinterest, her eyes moving from Ellie to the menu board behind her head.

"Nice to meet you, Whitney."

"And I'm Michael, Michael West." He moved into a position, blocking Ellie from his gaze, offering his hand to Hugo.

"Well, hello, Michael, wonderful to meet you. Michael, a common name. The Hebrew meaning is *who is like God*."

Michael liked the sound of that. He turned and winked at Ellie. "The man clearly knows his etymology."

The man's smile grew even larger. "A fellow wordsmith, and you clearly know fashion. I love that shirt, *champ*!" He made a growling noise and raked his hands out like claws at Michael. "It reminds me of the time I was in the jungles of Brazil being stalked by a jaguar. Just like the man-eating beast on your shirt."

"Oh yes, totally." Michael puffed up his chest.

"Michael," the man asked knowingly, "have you ever been to the Amazon?"

Michael hesitated. He'd fallen right into this boisterous man's trap. "No...," he answered softly. "Only the online store...."

"Clever! So, you've never been to the jungle?"

"I've been on a New York subway. I'm pretty sure that ticks off all the necessary boxes."

Hugo threw his head and laughed, his thick hair shaking like a lion's mane. "The famous, concrete jungle, just as dangerous indeed," he said thumping Michael's chest.

"So," Michael inquired, trying to steer the conversation away from where he *hadn't* been and what he *hadn't* done. "Are you guys visiting? New in town? Leaving soon?" he whispered under his breath.

"Both, actually. We just arrived last night, and let me tell you, Lana Cove is a little slice of heaven. We dined with Theodopolus Withers...at a little seaside restaurant, and let me tell you, what a lovely man. Anyways, he told us that this café was exceptional and that we should stop by for breakfast, that everyone was treated like family. So, here we are."

"Theodopolus? I'm sorry, I don't—"

"He's the owner of the Lana Cove Historical Society and Museum and quite the philanthropist," Ellie explained.

"Oh." Michael nodded. "Now it makes sense. "Wait…." He scrunched up his face. "Well, actually, it doesn't make sense."

"Whitney and I, along with my team, are here to begin the world tour of Baal, a famous Egyptian sorcerer, lost for centuries, and we found him and his treasures. I dare say that there hasn't been excitement like this in the archeological world since the great Tutankhamun was discovered in 1922."

"That's quite some claim."

"The find of the century, Michael," he exclaimed grandiosely. Hugo turned and addressed the café as if giving a performance. "Everyone should come to the exhibit. We'll be unveiling rare Egyptian artifacts hidden for a millennia, unseen by *anyone* in the world, except my team."

"Fascinating," Ellie said. "I'm sorry, I have to ask, you're launching a worldwide exhibit from…Lana Cove? I would have thought New York or Los Angeles would be a more appropriate venue."

"I understand. Lana Cove doesn't seem like the place you would launch a worldwide event. But it just so happens that Oscar Threadmore graciously funded the entire expedition, under the agreement, of course, that the exhibit would begin here."

Whitney shifted her feet and crossed her arms. She was quickly becoming bored with the conversation and Hugo's bloviating.

"That's incredible! Did you hear that, Michael? I dreamed of being an archeologist when I was young. There's something so mysterious about Egypt's past." Ellie blushed at her sudden admission. "I guess it's the magic and the intrigue…."

"Oh, my God," Whitney said, punctuating each word under her breath.

"I'm sorry, enough about me. I'm sure that you have a million things to get ready. What can I get you? It's on the house."

"Finally," Whitney mouthed, rolling her eyes.

Michael took a step back and scrutinized Hugo while he and his irritated companion ordered breakfast. He had to admit, the man certainly embraced the role of a famous archeologist. His safari-style shirt, precariously unbuttoned, exposed a golden necklace with some sort of Egyptian carving, and his khaki shorts stopped just above his knees, revealing tan, muscular calves.

Whitney glanced over at him and caught him staring. "Snap out of it." She smiled slyly. "He's all mine."

"Oh, no, no." Michael held out his hands. "I wasn't staring. My mind just wandered off—it does that all the time."

Whitney laughed at him, and then her gaze moved from him to Ellie, and then back to his eyes. A sudden look of understanding filled her face.

"Oh." She nodded, her face filled with delight, like she'd just caught Michael with his hand in the proverbial cookie jar. "I see. You're sizing up the competition, that whole *alpha male* thing."

She took a step toward Michael and held her hand up to her mouth and whispered, "I'm sorry, it was Michael, right?" She crinkled her tiny nose. "You're a bit out of your league."

Hugo thanked Ellie and turned to Whitney. "What are you two jabbering about?"

Whitney remained silent, so Michael adlibbed. "Just how happy we are to finally have a little excitement here in Lana Cove."

Out of the corner of his eye, Michael caught Mary Taylor's rose-colored lips mouthing the word *liar*.

Hugo grabbed Michael's hand in a bone-crushing vise grip. "We're thrilled to be here. I'm sure we'll be seeing a *lot* of each other."

"Wonderful to meet you, and Whitney as well," Michael groaned out. He dropped his hand to his side and wriggled his fingers painfully.

"Well, we're off to enjoy a bit of the gorgeous sunshine." Hugo nodded to Michael and then maneuvered with Whitney through the sea of tables, making his way outside to the old wooden deck, attached to the front of the café. When Michael turned back to Ellie, her face was aglow.

"How exciting!" she gushed. "A famous archeologist. I bet he has some amazing stories. We *have* to go to his exhibit."

"Yes," Michael agreed halfheartedly. "I can't wait." He hated himself for the feelings of jealousy that crept through him. "Speaking of exciting news, guess what I'm doing?"

"Honestly…," Ellie made an apologetic face, "…I'm afraid to ask."

"I'm taking classes at Seascape Investigations, to get my private investigator's license."

"Get out of town!"

Michael could tell from her reaction she was truly surprised. "Nope. I think it will help add that extra layer of reality to my novels."

"Novel," she teased.

"Yes, thank you for making me painfully aware of that. Novel, singular."

"I think that's great, Michael. You're really embracing your new life. I'm proud of you." Ellie grasped his hand and squeezed it. Her touch sent a jolt of electricity through him. "How is your shoulder feeling?"

It's not my shoulder that hurts right now. It's my hand after having it crushed by Hugo. But instead, he replied, "Getting better every day. You know," Michael said, glancing toward the deck, "I bet that guy Hugo has never taken a bullet to the chest."

Ellie cocked her head, scrunching her face. "If I were you...," she looked tenderly at Michael, "You're a great guy, I wouldn't go about trying to compare war stories with him."

"Yeah," Michael agreed, somber. "You're probably right. I wouldn't want to embarrass him."

"Exactly." She smiled. "He and his team being guests here in Lana Cove, and all."

"Well, Miss Banks," Michael sighed. "I better get on the road. I have a Skype call with an art conservator."

"Sounds fascinating."

"I know, right?" He put on his tortoiseshell sunglasses. "I need the inside scoop on forgeries for my book, and it turns out that art conservators also tend to be the best forgers."

"Maybe you'll find the secret story behind that shirt," she teased.

"The only secret about this shirt...," Michael winked, "...is what lies beneath."

Chapter 3

Bliss

Michael glided across the kitchen floor, the sleeves of his powder-blue shirt rolled up over his forearms. He leaned over the cutting board and, using his knife, scraped broccoli florets, diced yellow peppers, and crushed garlic into a large sauté pan.

He'd never had the luxury of cooking when he lived in Boston. His life before consisted of frozen dinners or dining out with clients. Now in his new house, he found the simple task of cutting vegetables, measuring ingredients, and following simple instructions to be organic, wholesome. Something about the entire process was incredibly fulfilling.

He grabbed a wooden spoon and mixed the chicken and golden-brown vegetables in the saucepan.

"That's absolutely heavenly," he sighed, breathing in the aroma.

He glanced at the chicken stir-fry recipe—three tablespoons of rice vinegar, two tablespoons of honey. He measured out the ingredients and stirred them into the saucepan. "Perfect!"

He was just about to pour himself a glass of Pinot Blanc when his cell phone rang. He dashed across the kitchen, wiped his hands off on his dishtowel, and picked up his phone. A number he didn't recognize appeared on the screen.

A surge of anger coursed through him, ruining his Zen cooking moment. He jabbed the answer button and then pressed the speaker icon.

"Hello," he answered, eyeing his saucepan, his voice conveying his annoyance at the interruption.

"Good evening," a male voice said, "am I speaking with Michael West?"

Michael hesitated. "May I ask who's calling?"

"Yes, this is Robert Jenkins, from Centennial Insurance Company."

"Hi, it was Robert, correct?" Michael turned his attention back to his stir-fry. "I already have excellent insurance—life, car, homeowner's, you name it—so I'm afraid you're wasting your time. Have a nice evening."

He was just about to press the end-call button when Robert said, "Mr. West, it's in regard to the stolen paintings."

Michael froze. "What about the paintings?" He continued stirring the vegetables and the chicken, his curiosity piqued.

"I'm calling on behalf of Sir Charles Ainsworth. He's the owner of the paintings and the *inverted* Jenny stamp that you recovered."

"Oh, yes. Please let Sir Charles know that I'm happy that they were returned to their rightful owner. They *were* returned, right?"

"Yes, returned and analyzed. Everything is just fine. Mr. West, the reason I'm calling you is Sir Ainsworth hired our company to facilitate the return of his artwork and to make sure that you received the reward for the return of those stolen items."

"Reward? I wasn't aware of a reward."

"Yes, all major works of art are insured, Mr. West. Now, I simply need to confirm your mailing address, or your bank account information. We can deposit the money directly into your account if you would like."

"My account? Can you give me one second, Robert? I apologize if I sound distracted, I was just in the middle of making dinner. Let me turn down the stove."

"Yes, of course," Robert replied. "Take your time."

Michael turned the stove to low, hurried through the kitchen into the living room, and flipped open the lid of his laptop. He was wary of giving anyone information over the phone. He typed in his password and launched his browser and Googled *Centennial Insurance Company*. He clicked the link and compared the phone number with the one displayed on his screen. After giving the company a quick perusal, Michael felt the call was legitimate.

"If you don't mind," Michael said, "a check would work much better for me. Also, just out of curiosity, how much of a reward are we talking about?"

"Fifty thousand dollars, Mr. West."

Michael was silent as the number settled in.

"If I could please confirm your mailing address," continued Robert, who Michael imagined was accustomed to paying out large sums of money, "I can get everything processed."

"Yes, certainly. Eleven-zero-eight Ocean Crest Lane. It's in Lana Cove, North Carolina."

"Thank you, Mr. West. I have the information on the claim report. I simply needed to verify your address." The *click-clack* of a keyboard filtered down the line. "We'll have the payment processed and out to you within the next two business days."

"Thank you, Robert. I'm glad I picked up the phone." Michael laughed.

"I am, too. Thank you, Mr. West. Enjoy your evening."

"You too." Michael stared at his phone in disbelief. *Fifty thousand dollars.... Imagine how many shirts I could buy.*

He walked back into the kitchen and tasted the stir-fry. *Delicious.* He added a pinch of salt and pepper and stirred it in. His stomach growled in anticipation. He placed the stirrer on the stove and stood with his hands on his hips, lost in thought.

"I'm going to split the reward," Michael declared. *The money is just as much Ellie's and Olivia's as it is mine.*

He grabbed a chilled wine glass and a bottle of Pinot Blanc from the refrigerator. The gentleman at the boutique grocer had recommended it as a fruity wine that paired perfectly with grilled chicken.

He picked up the phone and was about to call Ellie when he stopped himself. No, this was the kind of news you delivered in person. Both Ellie and Olivia had been extremely strapped for cash after opening the Bitter Sweet Café. Ellie had spent all of her savings; the reward money would certainly be helpful.

Michael scooped three large spoonful's of fluffy sticky rice into a bowl and then ladled the chicken stir-fry on top. He inhaled deeply, breathing in the rich blend of spices and grilled chicken. He turned off the stove and padded into the living room, settling onto the couch, his bowl of food in one hand and his glass of wine in the other.

He had to admit, this was the perfect night. He toyed with the idea of calling Ellie again, but no, he really wanted to see that beautiful smile when he told her the great news about the reward money. He imagined her arms around him, thanking him for his generosity.

He snatched up the remote and turned on the television. For now, he'd settle back and surf Netflix for a movie. Nothing could ruin his blissful evening—except for Hugo's large head, his perfect hair, his sculpted, rugged jaw, plastered on the TV screen. The scrawler across the bottom read: *Legendary Archeologist Discovers Rare Ancient Ruins.*

Michael sighed. Hugo was proving to be a worthy adversary.

Chapter 4

An Unwanted Gift

Michael parked his Miata and ran his fingers through his windblown hair. He shouldered the driver-side door open, climbed out, and closed it with his hip. A cool morning breeze swept across the parking lot, making the bottom of his shirt dance a hula around his waist. A brushstroke of clouds stretched in long wispy lines across the sky. It was another beautiful morning.

The silver bell above the doorway tinkled as he stepped inside the Bitter Sweet Café. He smiled and relaxed his shoulders. Everything seemed perfect. Arthur Wisely was blustering, Mary Taylor was lost in her mocha cappuccino, and REO Speedwagon was belting out their tragic love ballad from the '80s, "Can't Fight This Feeling."

Michael turned his attention from the dining area to the front counter. *Strange,* he thought, *Jeff's working the front counter.* He could never understand Ellie's reasoning for letting the thirty-something millennial work the register. He was usually the barista, hidden behind a cloud of smoke and steam.

Ellie didn't really have a uniform for her staff, but Jeff certainly had one. It usually consisted of black skinny jeans and a black-collared dress shirt. He hid a pair of intelligent eyes and an attractive face behind a mop of thick black hair.

Michael picked up on a curious oddity, a Mickey Mouse watch, with a simple brown leather band. Michael had only caught a glimpse of the watch once or twice because Jeff had quickly pulled his sleeve over it. Everything Jeff wore was black, from his shoes to his dyed black hair, but there was something unique about that watch, that splash of color hidden beneath his sleeve.

Michael had wanted to ask him about it, but something told him it was off-limits. He rarely listened to his inner voice of reasoning, but he listened this time.

"Good morning, Jeff, nice to see you." Michael smiled kindly.

"Morning, Michael." He cocked his head. "The usual?"

"Yes, and…." Michael leaned forward, checking the long, narrow corridor behind the counter for Ellie.

"I just cleaned that." Jeff shooed him back from the counter and shook his head as if scolding a child.

"Sorry." Michael snatched a napkin from the dispenser and wiped off the glass countertop. "I don't see Ellie or Liv—are they here today?" He leaned forward again, checking behind the counter, careful not to touch the glass.

"They're at the employee's table," Jeff replied, handing Michael his coffee.

"Thank you, Jeff, have a great day." But his words fell on deaf ears. The barista in black had already turned and walked away.

"No fancy tiger shirt today, Michael?" Mary Taylor teased as he passed by.

"It was a jaguar, Mary," Michael sighed. "Try to learn your big cats."

He took a sip of coffee and made his way to the end of the counter, pausing momentarily to admire a delectable stack of gooey fudge brownies. He made the sign of the cross with his fingers. "Get back, you vile temptress," he whispered to the brownies as he continued to the employee's table. A huge smile filled his face when he heard Ellie's bubbly laugh. He had to admit, it was one of his favorite sounds.

He turned the corner at the end of the counter, only to see Hugo, Ellie, and Olivia sitting at the table, tears of laughter streaming down Ellie's face. He was just in time to see Hugo shake the silverware from his napkin and then use it to dab away her tears.

Michael fell back onto his heels. He felt like he'd been sucker-punched in the heart. All of the air escaped his lungs. He took a step backward. Maybe he should just…. Olivia's eyes caught his, a smile flashed across her face, and then she must have seen Michael's expression and Hugo wiping Ellie's eyes. She immediately understood.

Olivia, Michael's friend and co-owner of the Bitter Sweet Cafe had known for months that Michael had feelings for Ellie, and truth be known, Ellie cared deeply for Michael, but she'd yet to pursue anything more than a close friendship with him. Still, seeing Michael's face, she must have known exactly what he was feeling.

Michael turned, vaguely aware of Mary and the other diners watching him. For a moment, he stood frozen, unsure of what to do. He couldn't just stand there and watch Hugo fawning over Ellie. He felt like an idiot. *Should I just leave and go home*? Or…. He glanced out the window, looking out onto the deck. His cozy nook in the corner had brought him solace through many trying days. *Maybe I'll sit outside in the sunlight and try to write*. He clutched his notepad and turned to leave.

Olivia came up behind him and grabbed him by the hand. "Michael." She smiled brightly. "We've *all* been waiting for you." She gave his hand a gentle tug. "Come on."

"I don't want to intrude." Michael hesitated. "You guys are—"

Hugo pushed back from the table, sending his chair skittering, and leaped to his feet. "Good morning, Michael."

"Good morning, Hugo, nice to see you," Michael lied.

"Nice to be seen." He laughed. "Ellie was just telling me about the time you got shot in the chest. I would have never guessed. Who do you think you are, James Bond?"

Here we go. "It wasn't that heroic. I was actually hiding in a drainage ditch when I got shot, not exactly James Bond-worthy."

"Nonsense." Hugo smacked Michael's shoulder, knocking him sideways. "I told her that my great white shark attack—off the coast of Australia—was nothing compared to the heroism you displayed. Although," he tilted his head, thinking, "the cobra bite in Malaysia…that one nearly took me away from this world." He pointed to a long fang dangling from his necklace. "Had this little darling dipped in gold to always remind me how precious life is."

"Now the snake probably talks with a lisp," Michael said dryly.

"What? Oh, clever, because he's only got one fang. That's funny—I'll have to remember that."

"You can tell the joke over fangs-giving," Michael added, unable to stop himself.

Olivia snickered behind her hand. *He's such an idiot.*

"You're a riot, Mr. West," Hugo laughed. "You should be a comedian."

"Thank you, Hugo." Michael tilted his head, acknowledging Hugo's compliment. "All right. Olivia, Ellie, wonderful to see you this morning. I'll let you guys get back to your meeting. I've got a lot of writing to do and a class at one-thirty."

"Class?" Olivia looked from Ellie back to Michael. "What class? You never told me you were taking a class."

"It's nothing." Michael held out his hands in surrender. He'd faced enough belittling for the day. "I shouldn't have even mentioned it."

Ellie's brow furrowed. "Michael, what's the matter with you?" She turned to Olivia. "He's taking a private investigator's class. I'm proud of him."

"You're going to become a private investigator? And you didn't bother telling me?" Olivia asked, clearly annoyed with being kept in the dark.

"It's not like that. I'm just doing it for research, you know, so my book can be more authentic."

"Very noble." Hugo nodded. "A man willing to go the extra mile to better his craft—you *have* to respect that."

"Thank you, Hugo, I appreciate that."

"Well, it takes a special kind of man to be a writer. I tried it once, but I just don't have the patience. I'm more of a 'grab the tiger by the tail' kind of man. I like to experience adventure." He arched his eyebrows at Ellie. "Rather than imagine it."

Michael didn't know whether to throw up or take notes. He was clearly being upstaged by Hugo's gargantuan ego.

"So," Olivia said, interrupting the awkwardness. "Hugo has brought three VIP passes to the exhibit tonight."

"That's right," Hugo exclaimed proudly. "It will only be a small crowd of distinguished guests: investors, close friends, and a few exclusive talents from various news agencies." Hugo snapped his fingers. "Maybe we can get some more exposure for your café," he offered Ellie and Olivia.

"The VIP tickets to the exhibit are enough," Ellie said.

Olivia nodded in agreement. "We're just grateful for the tickets and the invitation."

"All right, but if you change your mind...." He fished his phone out of his pocket and glanced at the screen. "Ah," he intoned, clucking his tongue. "Ladies, Michael, it looks like I'm needed at the museum. So…." He rubbed his hands together. "I'll see you tonight?" The question was addressed to the table, but his eyes were on Ellie.

"Of course," Olivia answered for everyone. "We wouldn't miss it for the world."

"Exquisite, and don't worry, Mr. Bond." Hugo grabbed Michael's shoulder. "I'll make sure your cocktails are shaken, not stirred."

Michael forced a smile. *I really hate this man.*

Chapter 5

The Curse of Baal

Michael climbed out of the back seat of the black BMW X5 and held the door open for Olivia. The Uber driver dashed from behind the wheel on the other side of the car to open the door for Ellie.

"Thank you, sir." Olivia offered her hand to Michael.

"My lady." He bowed and stepped back, giving her room.

Olivia looked stunning in a yellow strapless dress. Her golden hair fell in soft curls over her shoulders. She had a dusting of light-blue eyeshadow and a hint of gloss on her lips.

"You're absolutely beautiful." Michael smiled.

"Ah, Michael, you're gonna make me blush."

Ellie stepped around the front of the car and joined them.

"Ellie, you look absolutely gorgeous in that dress," Michael exclaimed as she joined them.

Ellie wore her hair up in a crown braid with soft wavy strands playfully falling along her cheeks, framing her face. Her black slip dress flowed over her, tastefully accentuating her slender body.

"Yes, she does!" Hugo stood several feet from her, arms spread. "A goddess. No, I stand corrected, two goddesses have graced us with their presence tonight."

"Thank you." Michael laughed, running his fingers through his hair. "Sorry, Ellie, maybe next time."

A small phalanx of photographers descended on them, snapping pictures. Hugo pulled Ellie in close for a series of photos.

"Where's your other half?" Michael piped up. It was spiteful, but someone needed to put the brakes on Hugo's infatuation with Ellie.

A momentary flash of confusion spread over Hugo's face, and then that smile—so powerful it could have been its own entity. "Oh, my assistant. She's inside working the exhibit."

"Whitney's been downgraded from his other half to his assistant in twenty-four hours," Michael whispered to Olivia.

"Don't mind him, my darling. Tonight is about adventure and magic. May I?" Hugo intertwined his arm through Ellie's and walked toward the entrance of the museum, photographers following him every step of the way.

Michael gave Olivia a look of disgust. "What is going on around here?"

"Don't ask me." Olivia slid her arm into the crook of Michael's. "What can I say? The girl likes archeology."

"But…," he said, staring, "I've never seen her act this way. She's always so…." He struggled for the word to complete his thought.

"Boring? Predictable? Careful what you say, Mr. West. Ellie's just having a good time. You're in your head too much. Relax, we *all* know that he's full of himself."

"Ellie may know it," Michael frowned, "but I'm not sure *he* does."

"Michael, you have a gorgeous woman on your arm who would like to have a fun evening."

"You're absolutely right, Olivia." Michael felt ashamed. "I'm acting like a buffoon. I'm a lucky man to have such wonderful friends."

"And…," Olivia prompted.

"A beautiful woman accompanying me." Michael smiled.

"That's better." Olivia snatched the tickets from him and handed them to a tall gentleman dressed in a black tuxedo attending the door.

"Allow me," the man said in an unexpected soft southern accent. He opened the door and deftly stepped aside so they could enter.

A cool wall of air-conditioning met them as they walked inside. An eclectic swirl of Egyptian music gave the air an electric vibe. A harp played, accompanied by a drummer and a flute, its breathy notes syncopated with each drumbeat.

A large blue-and-gold banner spanned the entrance of the museum. The words *The Forbidden World of the Dark Pharaoh* stretched across the length of it. Beneath the words was a photo taken at night using a blue filter, featuring a series of pyramids illuminated by a golden light. To the right of the pyramids was a scroll, surrounded by golden wisps of magic, and beneath the scroll were the words *The Book of the Dead*. The banner shimmered due to the blasting air-conditioner, seemingly bringing the scene to life.

"The Book of the Dead," Olivia said quietly, "probably not a bestseller."

"Maybe not a bestseller, but very popular. I did a little reading last night," Michael explained.

Olivia looked at him curiously. "Uh-huh," she teased, "a sudden fascination with Egyptian culture."

Michael ignored her dig and continued. "It seems the Egyptians had a strong belief in magic. The Book of the Dead was kind of their Fodor's travel guide to navigating the afterlife."

"Like merge left for Heaven, turn right for Hell, or stay in the straight lane for purgatory?"

"Something like that." Michael laughed. "It contains one hundred and ninety spells that are supposed to help the soul reach The Field of Reeds. Not to be confused with the *Field of Dreams*, where you'll end up at Kevin Costner's house."

"Could be worse," Olivia stated.

"Anyways, The Field of Reeds is supposed to be an eternal paradise without disease, disappointment, or the fear of death."

"Well, at least they seemed to be optimistic about death—none of the fire and brimstone ideologies."

"That was quite succinct." Michael laughed.

"My dad is a Southern Baptist preacher, and in his line of work you're either going up or down—there's no in-between."

Olivia and Michael arrived at a large cathedral-shaped room. A beautiful golden sarcophagus stood in the center. Deep-red and rich-blue designs covered its entirety. A golden band adorned with hieroglyphs wrapped around the base. Two columns with the golden bust of Anubis, the god of death, stood on opposite sides of the sarcophagus. A red velvet rope secured the area.

"It's beautiful," Olivia said, mesmerized by the complexity of the artwork covering the sarcophagus. "The colors remind me of the stained-glass windows I saw in the Siena Cathedral in Italy."

Dozens of glass display cases were nested against the walls, each one filled with Egyptian artifacts. Videos played above each display case, featuring Hugo, of course, explaining each find. Visitors were encouraged to download an app for their phones so they could watch the videos at their leisure.

The museum was filled with Lana Cove's rich and famous, the men dressed in their black suits, the women in their finest evening gowns. Michael recognized several locally renowned news hosts and various socialites.

To the far right of the exhibit's centerpiece stood a long table decorated in black silk with gold trimming. A man dressed as an Egyptian pharaoh made drinks, and women dressed like Egyptian royalty delivered them on golden trays to the attendees. An expresso station was set up next to it, the brown sugar cubes arranged in the shape of a pyramid.

Michael spotted Ellie, standing arm in arm with Hugo. They were speaking to a stout man with half-moon wisps of white hair over each ear and a small tuft of what looked like cotton candy on top. Even though the man was dressed in a perfectly tailored black tux, Michael could tell he was losing his battle with gravity.

"Who is that?" Michael tilted his head toward the rotund man.

"I believe that's Oscar Threadmore, the guy who bankrolled Hugo's expedition."

"Oh…well, at least Ellie's getting to hobnob with some of Lana Cove's social elite," Michael said.

"Yes, however, I think she has made herself an enemy."

Michael followed Olivia's gaze. Whitney was standing next to a man, a glass of red wine in her hand, staring daggers at Ellie. Michael guessed the man was her colleague. He had a deep tan that could only come from spending hours in the sun. His brown hair was cut short, receding a bit over the temples. One eyebrow arched slightly upward above his nose, making him appear instantly trustworthy or concerned. *He'd either make a great salesman or a politician.* He, too, was looking at Hugo and Ellie, shaking his head.

"That is the face of a woman scorned," Michael observed.

"Sounds like the voice of experience." Olivia smiled.

"I think every man innately knows that expression," Michael acknowledged.

"I don't know why she stays with him—I certainly wouldn't."

"Maybe she hopes he'll change," Michael offered.

Olivia shook her head. "Men like that never change, Michael. They just keep collecting shiny things."

A tall, thin man glided across the floor and joined Hugo's trio. His wire-framed oval glasses were much too small for his long face, giving him the appearance of an insect. He stroked a silvery-white goatee as he fell into conversations with Oscar and Hugo.

"That's Theodopolus Withers," Olivia explained. "He's the museum curator."

"Just how I'd imagined a museum curator," Michael replied. A spark of jealousy flew through him: Hugo put his arm around Ellie and introduced her to the group's newest arrival.

Oscar Threadmore glanced over his shoulder at the crowd. He turned back and whispered something into Hugo's ear and then strode to the center of the room.

"Good evening, everyone." He spoke with a deep, resonating voice. He waited a moment for the attendees to quiet down and give their attention to him.

"For those of you who don't know me…." He gave a smile that said *if that's even possible*. "…I'm Oscar Threadmore, the philanthropist behind this amazing expedition."

Oscar opened his arms in self-adulation, clearly enjoying the brief smattering of applause that filled the room.

"Thank you, thank you." He nodded ingratiatingly. "When Hugo approached me with the exciting news that he had received a mysterious tip that could lead to one of the most important historical finds of the century, I jumped at the opportunity to play an integral part of this fabulous adventure."

He paused dramatically as if searching his soul for his next thought.

"And…." He smiled tenderly. "I must say, I've never made a better decision in my life. Well, except for marrying my beautiful bride, Ingrid."

He turned and toasted a woman who was obviously flirting with the shirtless pharaoh serving drinks. She recovered quickly and raised a glass to him, mouthing, *I love you, darling.*

A disgruntled look flashed across his face. It was quickly replaced with an air of self-importance. "Where was I? Oh, yes." He directed his focus back to the crowd. A small group of photographers huddled nearby, snapping photos.

"Tonight is an exciting night for all of us. Hugo Sebastian's expedition far surpassed anything I could have ever hoped for. He discovered...." Oscar paused mid-sentence. "Folks, I'm going to do something I rarely do, and that's relinquish the spotlight."

A polite laugh rose from the audience.

"While it's true that I spent a vast fortune making the expedition and this event possible...."

"His modesty is palatable," Michael whispered.

"I believe that the world-famous archeologist, Hugo Sebastian, should tell you about this miraculous discovery."

Oscar waved him over. Hugo, always the entertainer, made a huge production of acting surprised. He touched his chest as if to ask, *Me?* He excused himself from Ellie and Theodopolus and made his way to Oscar, nodding his appreciation as the audience applauded.

"Thank you so much, Oscar." He placed a hand on his shoulder. "You know, my friend, none of this would have been possible without you."

Oscar smiled and awkwardly patted him on the arm. "Mr. Hugo Sebastian." He waved goodbye to the crowd and then scuttled away to rescue his wife from the clutches of the shirtless pharaoh.

Hugo paused for another smattering of applause. "Thank you, thank you, everyone. Distinguished guests, tonight you will have the privilege of seeing the face of Baal."

Hugo gestured reverently toward the sarcophagus. The museum lights dimmed, and a single spotlight illuminated the gleaming golden sarcophagus. Excited *oohs* and *ahs* emanated from the audience.

"Unknown to most," Hugo continued dramatically, "Baal was Egypt's most feared sorcerer."

Above the mummy, a screen came to life, a pharaoh materialized, and then an artist's rendition of a sorcerer, his eyes hypnotic.

"Ancient writings and paintings described Baal's powers as godlike."

There was a peal of thunder, and lightning flashed across the screen.

"No man, or ruler, could look upon his face without the fear of death."

An image of Baal appeared on the screen, his hand stretched out. On his knees in front of him, a man was clutching at his throat, his face in the throes of agony.

"Unless you had…."

Another spotlight burst to life, illuminating Hugo. He paused dramatically and then slowly unbuttoned the top two buttons of his shirt. A soft whistle emanated from someone in the audience.

Hugo cocked an eyebrow and smiled. "Someone has good taste."

Michael seriously considered impaling Hugo with one of the spears that hung behind him. Surely the police would understand.

Hugo slipped his hand inside his shirt and revealed a golden necklace. He let it dangle over the palm of his hand so everyone could see. A jeweled amulet glistened brightly in the spotlight.

"I wonder if he has a different necklace for each story," Michael whispered into Olivia's ear.

"Michael, hush," she exclaimed under her breath.

"The amulet that I wear tonight is over thirty-two centuries old. It is the royal amulet, given to Ramesses the second, by Baal himself. It contains the ashes of his predecessor. Only the wearer of this amulet can stare into the eyes of Baal without dying."

He turned so everyone could get a closer look. The photographers inched in closer, their cameras whirring and clicking.

"Hugo," a voice called out from the darkness. "Aren't you a bit old to believe in sorcery and wizardry?"

A smattering of laughter flitted throughout the room.

"Now's the part where he brushes back his bangs, revealing a scar in the shape of a lightning bolt on his forehead," Michael whispered.

Olivia raised up on her toes, scanning the crowd for the brave soul who dared to call out Hugo the Great.

Emboldened by the limelight, the man took a step forward from the scrum of photographers. He smiled smugly, enjoying the sudden attention.

"Hugo." He held his slender hands against his chest. "I mean no disrespect. Your commitment and accomplishments in the archeological field are noteworthy, but...this feels cheap." He shook his head as if admonishing a child. "Seriously, a magical amulet, death from someone staring at you? Come on."

Oscar handed his drink to his wife, gave the shirtless pharaoh a dark look, and briskly walked toward Hugo. He wasn't about to let some miscreant ruin their grand opening.

A broad smile spread across Hugo's face. He licked his lips hungrily.

"If someone would please raise the main lights," Hugo called out, "I would like to see who I'm addressing."

The overhead lights came to life, illuminating the room.

"I'm Ivan Ware," a young man breaking from the crowd said. "*Washington Post*," he stated proudly.

"Well, welcome, Ivan." Hugo took in the man in front of him.

His hair was gathered atop his head in a loose man bun, his eyes set wide apart across a thin nose. A sole patch of reddish-brown hair extended from beneath his lip to the bottom of his chin. His long, thin fingers were wrapped around an expensive-looking camera.

"The *Washington Post* is a fine newspaper. I'm glad you could attend our little soirée. To answer your question, no, one is never too old to believe in the truth."

"So, you're telling us," he gestured to the crowd, "that you believe Baal could kill someone by staring into their eyes."

"Yes," Hugo replied, "or by cursing them." He became aware of Oscar's hand on his shoulder.

"Don't worry, I'll have him ushered out," he whispered into Hugo's ear.

"No. No." Hugo patted Oscar's hand. "He has a right to be here, and his questions are well-founded. He's fine."

Oscar nodded hesitantly, clearly uncomfortable with the turn of events.

Ivan shook his head. "I must say that I'm disappointed. I came here with the expectation of a monumental historic find. Instead, you've discovered yet another mummy, and you've created a phantasmal story about a sorcerer named Baal. Feels like you're simply trying to fatten your backstory and your wallet, at the expense of all of us." He knelt to the floor and put his camera away. "What a waste of time."

"Ivan, before you leave, would you be so kind as to let me explain myself? I think you owe me that much. I mean, after your sudden outburst and accusations."

Ivan threw the strap of his camera case over his shoulder. "Honestly, I can't believe we are having this conversation."

"I'll keep my explanation brief. I was going to save this speech for the unveiling, but since you need answers, I'll oblige. Mr. Ware, quickly, what is your background? Do you have any scientific training?"

"No. I have a degree in media and journalism from Georgetown, and I've won numerous awards for—"

"Okay, we get the idea. So, your entire argument is based on your beliefs, your experiences, not science. Is that fair to say?"

"Yes." He snorted. "And yours is based on fantasy and magic. I'm sorry, but like most adults, I don't believe in fairytales."

"Nor do I," Hugo agreed. "But I do believe that Baal and others killed people—not by magic, but through fear."

"And that's where you take a little ride on a train to fantasy land." Ivan shook his head.

Hugo's eyes narrowed; his expression changed. His smile was still there, but there was something more menacing in his posture, the way he moved. Ivan must have sensed the transition and moved his camera in between himself and Hugo.

Hugo took another step toward Ivan. "Mr. Ware, are you saying you don't believe that fear can kill?"

Ivan stared curiously at Hugo, perhaps disoriented by his sudden change in behavior.

"Wouldn't it be nice, *Ivan*, if scientific reasoning was awarded to the loudest voice in the room? No more experimentation needed; theories simply substantiated by a person's gut?" He slammed his fist into his hand.

The audience gasped. Hugo took another step toward Ivan. He looked like a jaguar about to pounce.

Oscar leaned in and touched Hugo's elbow. "I think this has gone far enough," he warned.

"One moment, my friend," Hugo whispered. "Ivan, you thought you would humiliate me in front of my friends, my peers." He took another step forward and leaned into Ivan's space.

Ivan took a step back, his eyes flashing with fear. Michael could tell he wanted to stand his ground, but now a sheen of sweat had broken out over his forehead. His chest rose and fell rapidly.

"Calm down, Hugo," Ivan demanded, his voice shaking.

"You want to see if a curse could kill someone?" Hugo grinned evilly. "I'm going to prove to you that it can!" He slammed his foot onto the marble floor. The sound echoed through the museum like a gunshot.

Excited gasps and screams escaped the crowd.

Ivan scrambled backward, stumbling over his own feet, falling to the floor. He scrambled upright. "You're a fraud!" Ivan screamed, red-faced, shaking his fist. "I'll destroy you, just wait!" He stormed through the museum, shoved the main doors open, and disappeared into the night.

"Fascinating," Hugo declared excitedly, clasping his hands.

The small crowd stared at Hugo dumbfounded, a look of *What just happened?* and disbelief etched across their faces.

"Simon," Hugo called out. "If you would, please collect Mr. Ware. I would hate for him to miss out on the reveal because of an impassioned outburst."

Simon nodded and hurried through the museum, chasing after Ivan.

Chapter 6

Voodoo Death

Simon returned, shaking his head at Hugo, making it known that Ivan will not return. Hugo shrugged and returned his attention to the crowd.

"Everyone in this room just participated in a social experiment," Hugo explained, "all based on your perception. Mr. Ware, unintentionally, provided us with the perfect introduction to the magic of Baal. "Frightening, right? Although none of it was real. However, the tension, the anxiety that you all felt was." Hugo walked along the edge of the audience, reconnecting with them, smiling and engaging them.

"Remember when I said Baal killed through fear?"

The audience responded by nodding.

"Tonight, I'm going to give you a brief history and psychology lesson, and then…." He turned toward the sarcophagus, "…you will all meet Baal. Just like each of you, over the past few minutes, Mr. Ware went through some physiological changes. You probably experienced a few yourself." Hugo smiled apologetically at the audience.

"Mr. Ware's brain and body betrayed him. His breathing, his posture…he began to sweat and tremble. Did I ever touch him? Was I truly going to assault the man? Never, but this educated man was driven over the edge when I stomped my foot.

"This, my friends, is how Baal killed, how voodoo practitioners kill and how witch doctors kill. Ivan barely knew me, but in a short time, I was able to change his physiology by changing my behavior.

"If Mr. Ware had stayed, I would have shared with him the research done by Dr. Walter Cannon, chairman of the Harvard Department of Physiology. Dr. Cannon wrote a medical research paper entitled 'Voodoo Death,' where he documents case after case of people dying, simply by being cursed. "I know, I know," he said, seeing bemused smiles in the audience.

"Imagine a highly respected doctor writing about such a taboo topic. One would think it would be professional suicide. But, his paper was embraced by the medical community. His paper found that if a person believed that another person had significant power over whether they lived or die, they could kill you by cursing you.

"Baal had that power. He came from a long lineage of sorcerers. In Dr. Cannon's research paper, he examines numerous case studies done by anthropologists and doctors living among natives in South America, Africa, New Zealand, and Haiti, who have seen people die after being cursed by a witch doctor or medicine man. Do I believe it's magic? No. But I do believe that people can be scared to death. How do the people actually die? The phenomenon is called psychosomatic death. It's sudden death brought on by a strong emotional shock—in this case, fear. The human brain is an amazing tool, but it can be manipulated with dire results.

"Baal understood the power of belief. He understood the Egyptians' total acceptance of spells and curses—after all, this is what guided them to the afterlife. His dark magic was considered so powerful that three generations of Ramesses maintained his *forced* employment as their royal sorcerer. There are dozens of documented cases of men dying at the hands of Baal.

"Now, you've been patient enough. If you would bear with me for just one more moment, I would like to quickly introduce my team, and then, the grand event!"

Chapter 7

An Unfortunate Update

Whitney and Simon joined Hugo, standing on either side of him like bookends. Hugo turned and introduced Whitney first.

"This beautiful young woman is Whitney Cooper. She's been an integral part of my team for three years. She has advanced degrees in biology, chemistry, and...she is also an expert in herbal medicine."

Whitney mouthed a gracious thank you as the attendees applauded.

"And this is my right-hand man, Simon Parker." Hugo patted the man's back. "Simon's been a part of the team for five years. We've traveled the globe together. He has advanced degrees in anthropology and chemistry, and before I snatched him up, he was developing his own software for analyzing archeological finds. He's clearly a renaissance man."

Behind him, two technicians dressed in white jumpsuits and blue latex gloves wheeled the sarcophagus away from the wall. A cantilevered radiolucent table was maneuvered behind the mummy. A technician locked the wheels, and then together they slowly lowered Baal onto the table.

The crowd pressed in closer, whispering to each other.

"Hugo, over here." A fresh-faced gentleman waved. His dark hair was slicked back in an extreme part. "Joel Owens." He gave a friendly smile. "*New York Times*. You said that there is a curse if we stare into Baal's eyes, and, well, none of us have that fancy amulet you're wearing to protect ourselves."

"That's a good point," Michael agreed. "I need to live at least another twenty-five years so I can collect social security."

"Such profound aspirations," Olivia teased.

"Excellent point, Joel," Hugo agreed. "There is no need for alarm. We have placed a lead-infused cloth over his eyes. Which brings up an interesting point. When people go through the mummification process, their internal organs are removed. Their eyes are usually replaced with linen or stones. However, in Baal's case, his eyes are still there, covered by a clear resin.

"But again, for those of you who are superstitious, and for insurance reasons," he winked, "we have covered his eyes to guarantee your safety."

Simon walked briskly to the back of the room and disappeared into a hallway. Moments later, he returned pushing what looked like a giant white donut toward the sarcophagus.

Hugo glanced over his shoulder and then turned back to address his audience.

"We've spared no expense in bringing you the most advanced technology. This, my dear friends…," he motioned to the large machine Simon was wheeling into place, "…is a portable CT scanner. This imaging technology will allow us to peel away the layers of linen, revealing a 3D image of what lies beneath."

A technician helped Simon position the scanner in front of the sarcophagus, and then slowly pushed the top of the coffin into the scanner.

"So, a little secret. I've only seen Baal's remains through a portable x-ray device in Egypt. You and I will be seeing beneath his linen wrapping for the first time since he was buried. Imagine, we will be the first people to gaze upon the face of Baal in over two thousand years."

"But you have seen the mummy, right?" a woman asked. "I mean, there *is* a mummy in the sarcophagus." She laughed nervously.

"Of course," Hugo said, addressing her. "The sarcophagus was sealed in Egypt, flown by private jet under my supervision, hand-processed through customs, and brought directly to the museum, where it has been under twenty-four-hour surveillance since its arrival."

The woman smiled appreciatively. "Thank you."

A technician wheeled in a workstation, consisting of a large monitor and keyboard. He plugged in the computer, then taped the power cord to the floor. Another team of men maneuvered four barriers around the sarcophagus.

Disgruntled faces filled the crowd as the barriers were fitted together, blocking their view.

"Don't worry," Hugo reassured the audience, sensing their anxiety. "Those are lead barriers to protect us from any radiation emitted from the scanner. "Everyone will have a live view of the mummy on the screen."

Just as he described what was about to take place, the screen behind him flashed to life. It was divided into two sections. One half showed live video as to what was going on behind the protective barriers; the other half was a live feed from the CT scanner, which presently read *offline.*

There was a powerful *whooshing* sound as the scanner whirred to life. Hugo paced nervously back and forth in front of the barriers; the excitement was palatable.

The computer booted up at Simon's workstation, loading the enhanced Samsung imagery software. Everyone's attention was directed at the screen. Waiting to see Baal, the dark sorcerer.

Simon hunched over the terminal and then glanced up nervously. He motioned to one of the technicians. The man hurried over to join him. He stared at the monitor, asked Simon a couple of questions, shook his head, and then stared back at the console. Hugo must have sensed there was a problem and hurried over.

"Simon," Hugo hissed, "what's going on?"

"One second," Simon said under his breath. He shut down the system and rebooted.

Hugo was beside himself. "You said you tested everything!"

"I *did*," Simon replied angrily. "Everything was perfect this morning, but now it's saying that there is a mandatory software update, or else the equipment could be damaged."

"Well, then update it, and hurry!" Hugo ordered angrily.

Simon stared at him, clearly exasperated. "What do you think I'm trying to do? I'm looking to see if there's a manual override or another workaround," he insisted.

"How long does the software update take?"

Simon prepared himself. "It can take up to two hours."

"What?" Hugo nearly screamed. He clenched his teeth and inhaled sharply through his nose. "Two hours. Are you mad?" He grabbed Simon's arm and squeezed.

Simon winced as Hugo dug his fingers into the soft underside of his arm.

"You listen to me. We have people from all over the world here, and you're telling me it could take two hours? Fix it *now*!" he growled through clenched teeth.

"I'll try rebooting the system again," Simon replied, yanking his arm from Hugo's grasp. He ran his fingers through his hair in frustration. "You need to calm down—you're acting like an idiot. I don't control when they decide that a software update is needed."

"I don't want excuses. If you can't figure it out, find someone who can. The success of the event is on *your* shoulders!"

Chapter 8

Revenge

Ivan paced angrily around the parking lot. *How dare that pompous idiot humiliate me in front of my peers!* "I will destroy you," he growled to himself.

He opened the black leather satchel attached to the side of his Ducati Panigale motorcycle and stored his camera equipment and digital recorder. *I'm going to make sure that everyone sees the real Hugo Sebastian,* he thought to himself. He climbed onto his motorcycle, turned the key, and pressed the start button. The powerful V4 engine roared to life.

He loved the way the motorcycle felt beneath him, the throaty grumble of the exhaust, the raw power. He pulled back on the throttle; the bike responded with a roar. He slid his helmet on and walked his bike back out of the parking lot. He tore off across the parking lot, his mind racing like the motorcycle's engine. He smiled a hidden smile beneath his helmet. He would have his revenge.

Chapter 9

Postponed

Simon's face was covered in sweat. No matter what he tried, the software update would not load. The live video screen showed his repeated failed attempts, adding to his anxiety.

To avoid a PR disaster, Hugo beckoned the audience to him. "I'm sorry." He grinned broadly. "But as you can see, we are experiencing a wee bit of technical difficulty. Sometimes new discoveries require a little patience. In the meantime, as we sort this out, please have another drink, enjoy the hors d'oeuvres, and take in some of the amazing artifacts on display from our expedition. Whitney will be happy to answer any questions you may have."

Whitney gave Hugo an icy stare that should have frozen the blood of any mere mortal. Hugo in turn beamed at her, and then spun on his heel and walked away.

Oscar and Theodopolus caught up to Hugo at the workstation, their faces filled with concern.

"What's going on?" Theodopolus demanded. He looked out at the guests, who milled about impatiently.

"Software update," Hugo said exasperatedly.

"Now?" Oscar moaned. "Can't this wait?"

"It won't let us—"

"How long is this supposed to take?" Oscar asked, interrupting Simon.

Hugo fought back a wave of anger; his lips stretched tight across his face. "Simon said it could take a couple hours."

Oscar and Theodopolus gasped.

"I've spent thousands on this event," Oscar declared. "The media's here, for God's sake. If you can't get this to work, you're going to have to open that darned fancy casket."

"Whoa, Oscar, relax for a moment." Hugo grabbed the man's shoulder. "I know you've invested a lot, and believe me, the paybacks will be huge." He held Oscar's gaze. "You're going to have to trust me—I have a plan brewing."

Michael watched the trio's animated gestures. He could tell that things weren't going well. His gaze traveled to Simon, whose head was cocked forward, staring down at the screen, his phone cradled between his cheek and shoulder. *He must be calling tech support,* Michael thought.

"Michael." Olivia nudged him. "Check out Whitney."

Whitney was nestled in a corner, staring daggers at Ellie. She held her phone in such a way that Michael could tell she was either taking pictures of Ellie or videoing her as she grabbed a glass of wine from the shirtless pharaoh.

"Is she taking pictures of her?" Olivia asked.

"I think so," Michael replied. "And no, I have no idea why."

Ellie, drink in hand, turned and scanned the room. A smile washed across her face as she spotted Olivia and Michael in the crowd. She held out her drink and gestured to the pharaoh, mouthing the words, "Would you like another drink?"

"Did she just say what do you think?" Michael asked, dismayed, "because I think the Pharaoh's outfit is tasteless."

"No, she said, 'Would you like another drink?'" Olivia explained. She shook her head and held up her glass, showing Ellie it was still half full.

Michael gazed at Ellie as she walked across the floor, her dress accentuating her every move. Strands of hair danced across her cheeks. She was so beautiful, so elegant. His heart beat in time with her footsteps.

"This is so exciting," Ellie exclaimed, to no one in particular, her brown eyes aglow. "I hope they get the scanner working. And that confrontation," she quickly added before anyone could speak. "You could have heard a pin drop."

"Do you think it was staged?" Michael asked. "You know, to add a little excitement and mystique to Baal?"

"I don't think so," Olivia replied. "That guy was sweating so much he looked like he'd run through a sprinkler."

"Yeah, I guess." Michael nodded. "He just seemed a little over-the-top angry."

"Wouldn't you be if someone humiliated you in front of your peers?" Ellie asked.

"I never would have put myself in that position," Michael replied. "He had to know that it was going to end badly."

"Hugo may have gone a little overboard with the showmanship," Olivia suggested.

"A little? It was like watching a reality show," Michael said.

"He was trying to be entertaining. Remember how space launches used to be so exciting? Everyone would gather around the television; the astronauts would wave and make cheesy jokes. That's all gone. Now launches are an afterthought, covered by some obscure cable network." Ellie quickly shut her mouth and looked around, afraid she may have offended one of the cable news reporters milling about.

"I know what you're saying," Michael agreed. "It's an archeological find. He was trying to build up excitement and intrigue surrounding the discovery, and the only way to do that is to give people a show."

"Nevertheless," Ellie concluded, "Ivan thought he was trying to mislead the public, and in the end, he'll get his revenge. It's too easy to obliterate people online, where the other person can't fight back."

"I think Hugo is about to get more bad news." Michael nodded toward the group of men surrounding Simon.

Oscar, Theodopolus, and Hugo had converged on Simon, who jabbed at his phone; Michael imagined he was explaining he was getting help via his phone. Hugo smacked Simon's hand, sending his cell phone skittering across the floor. Michael lunged out and stopped it with his foot. He held the phone up, letting Simon know he had it.

Thank you, Simon mouthed silently.

Hugo and Simon faced off—it looked like they were going to come to blows. Then Hugo turned on his heel, and, like Moses parting the Red Sea, he separated Oscar and Theodopolus and stepped between them, making his way to the center of the room.

"Ladies and gentlemen." Hugo tried to smile, but for the first time since Michael had met him, it didn't reach his eyes. "As everyone can tell, we are having technical difficulties. A mandatory system update has decided to run at the most inconvenient of times."

Hugo took in a calming breath and slowly released it. The event that had held so much promise had become a nightmare. He could see, feel the disappointment that surrounded him.

"What does that mean *exactly*?" a smartly dressed woman in a black pencil skirt asked.

The silence was deafening, overwhelming. "It means that you will be unable to see Baal tonight. I am told that the update could take hours."

Hugo felt the woman's bitter displeasure like a knife to the heart. First the argument with Ivan, then the fight with Simon, and now he was unable to fulfill the promise he'd made to all these important people.

Hugo finally found his voice. "Listen, everyone. Before you text your producers or post to social media...," Hugo took a breath, "...I have a proposal for all of you that I think you will find most accommodating."

The room grew silent. Hugo looked out over the crowd. Every eye was on him.

"I cannot open the sarcophagus tonight." Hugo could barely get the words out of his mouth. "Tomorrow night is the official grand opening of the exhibit. I would like to invite each one of you—"

"Why can't you just open the sarcophagus tonight? You were going to do the CT scan," the woman inquired, her voice bitter.

"Ma'am," Hugo replied softly, "that's an excellent question, and if you would give me just a moment, I'll explain. The sarcophagus is secured by two Egyptian government seals." He gestured to the live video image of the sarcophagus. "They have been in place since we left Egypt. Two diplomats from the Egyptian government will join me tomorrow night to cut through the seals. So, to answer your question, it would be highly inappropriate to open the coffin without them being present."

"So, your compromise is to have us attend the grand opening with the general public? Hardly sounds like a compromise to me," the woman surmised.

Hugo pushed back a wave of anger. He was really beginning to dislike this woman. She seemed to enjoy stirring the pot, upsetting the guests. He smiled at the woman. "If you wish, you can leave. I'll make arrangements to cover the cost of your stay and transportation. However, if I were you, I would wait to hear my proposal before you make a decision."

Hugo turned and motioned Theodopolus and Oscar. He waited a moment for them to join him and then continued. "To make amends for a catastrophic dress rehearsal, tomorrow night, I would like each of you to arrive twenty minutes before the doors open. Each of you will be ushered in and seated in a special section surrounding the sarcophagus. You will be cordoned off, separated from the general public. You will be the first to see the unveiling of Baal. Not only that, but I am sure Mr. Withers will agree to my request: The museum will waive the ban on photographing and videoing of Baal. Exclusive only to my special guests, here tonight."

Theodopolus's face paled; Hugo had put him in a position where he couldn't say no. He nodded and waved in agreement to Hugo's speech.

A wave of excitement filled the air. Hugo felt the wave and decided to ride it. "Imagine," he said, the luster of the moment emboldening him. "You will be the first to see Baal. Your photos will be the first images of the mighty sorcerer the world has ever seen. This, my friends, is what I'm offering. A once-in-a-lifetime experience. Remember, a find like this happens once a century."

Silence encompassed the museum. Hugo took a breath; he felt like his heart had stopped beating. Then slowly like a flickering spark becoming a fire, the applause spread throughout the room. Hugo had done it.

"So…." He turned his attention to the woman who had been bent on wreaking havoc. "Will you be attending, or will I be covering your travel expenses?"

"I'll be attending," she answered sternly.

A broad smile spread across Hugo's face. "Thank you. It wouldn't be the same without you."

Chapter 10

Three's a Crowd

"My toes are killing me," Olivia moaned. "I'm not used to wearing heels."

"Feeling the same way," Michael agreed, wiggling his toes. "I haven't worn loafers for months. It's ten o'clock." He sighed as he looked at his watch. "I wonder how much longer Ellie's going to be?"

"She knows we're waiting. I'm sure she won't be much longer."

Olivia and Michael stood near the main entrance. The event had ended, and the main gallery was empty now, except for Whitney and Simon. Ellie had accompanied Hugo and Theodopolus to the administrative wing of the museum to secure a set of VIP security passes for the following night.

Simon yanked the control console's electric cord from the wall and wheeled it behind the donut-shaped CT scanner. He knelt below the sarcophagus and released the wheel locks at the base of the table, where the mummy lay, and pushed Baal down the same darkened corridor Ellie had gone down. Whitney lingered behind in the main gallery, busying herself at one of the display cases.

The tinkle of Ellie's laughter reached Michael before he saw her. He glanced over his shoulder. She and Hugo were making their way into the main exhibit area. Hugo took a step back from Ellie, grasped her hand, and kissed it. Ellie shook her head and laughed.

Whitney tore herself from the display—it was maybe more than she could take. She stepped in between Ellie and Hugo.

"Are you coming back to the hotel? I'm exhausted." She threw her hands down by her sides.

"Yes, of course. I was just getting Miss Banks and her friends VIP passes for tomorrow."

"I would like to leave now," Whitney demanded.

"Easy there." Hugo brushed her hair from her shoulder. "Simon and I have a few more things to wrap up before we leave. You go ahead." He grabbed her hand. "I'll be there shortly."

Whitney yanked her hand away. "How am I supposed to get back to the hotel?"

Hugo, unfazed, dug his hand into his pants pocket and handed her a set of keys. "I'll take an Uber back to the hotel." He smiled. "Don't wait up."

Whitney inhaled sharply, spun on her heels, and shouldered past Ellie.

"Wait, Whitney," Ellie called out, "we can give you a ride back to your hotel."

"You've done enough," Whitney spat. "Leave me alone." She disappeared down the hallway marked "Administration Offices."

Ellie followed for a few steps, then turned back to Hugo. "I think you better patch things up with Whitney. We'll see you tomorrow night." Ellie chose her words carefully. "Thank you for the tickets."

"My pleasure," nodded Hugo. He placed his hands in his pockets as he watched Ellie walk away.

Chapter 11

Eavesdrop

The black Uber Lincoln Navigator had just pulled out of the parking lot when Ellie panicked. "My purse! I left my purse inside."

"Not a worry," the driver said. He made a U-turn and drove back into the parking lot.

"Thank you so much," she said. "I'm terribly sorry."

"It's fine." The driver smiled as he eased up to the curb. "You're my last pickup of the evening. Take your time."

"Do you want me to go with you?" Olivia asked.

"No, you guys wait here, I'll be right back." Ellie pushed the door open and hurried up the steps to the museum. Her high heels *clicked* and *clacked* as she ascended. She'd just reached for the door handle when the door flew open, nearly knocking her off the landing. She staggered backward, regaining her balance.

"What are you doing here?" Whitney shrieked. Her eyes widened. "Oh, I see. Now I know why Hugo was working late." She literally spat the words at Ellie.

"No, no," Ellie exclaimed emphatically. "I forgot my purse. I was just running inside to get it."

Whitney blocked the doorway, holding her arm across the opening.

"Look, there is *nothing* between me and Hugo. I was just having fun. However, after I saw the way he treated you tonight…," Ellie lowered her eyes.

"Oh, spare me." Whitney shook her head in disgust. "Go get your," she held up her hands and made air quotes, "purse." She held the door in a way that made Ellie have to squeeze past her to get inside.

Ellie half stumbled into the doorway. The quick *tap, tap* of Whitney's high heels as she ran down the steps rang out behind her. The museum was quiet, the Egyptian music no longer filling the air. The only sound was the purring of the air-conditioning system. Ellie made her way into the main hall. The interior was dark. Only small banks of light illuminated the area, creating long shadows that stretched like black puddles across the floor.

She quickly crossed the exhibit area into the administrative hallway. The noise from her shoes seemed incredibly loud, intrusive. She froze. She could hear Hugo's voice further down the hall. He was angry, screaming at someone. Then she heard another voice—*Simon,* she concluded.

Ellie hurried down the hallway and stopped in front of a door simply marked A2. "Please be unlocked," she whispered as she reached for the doorknob.

Another bout of yelling broke the silence, followed by the sound of something crashing into the wall.

The doorknob twisted in her hand. Ellie pushed the door open and rushed inside. She sighed in relief—her silver clutch was lying on the table where she'd left it. She snatched it from the table, draped it over her shoulder, and headed for the door.

"Well, you scanned it before the event," Hugo shouted. "Where are those images?"

Ellie paused in the doorway and poked her head out. Not seeing anyone, she slipped into the hallway, quietly closing the door behind her. She winced as the locking mechanism clicked loudly. Ellie hesitated. She knew she shouldn't eavesdrop, but....

"We've been over this a dozen times," Simon's voice rang out. "I can't access them right now while it's updating."

"You're lying. I know you printed a copy," Hugo berated him.

"I didn't. Those were calibration tests. We didn't print anything because you were afraid someone would hack our system. Remember, it wasn't encrypted, and you were afraid someone would get the pictures and spread it to the news before our big reveal."

"All right." Hugo seemed to be calming down.

"Why are you so fixated on pictures?"

"I don't like surprises, Simon."

"What's that supposed to mean?"

Ellie whirled around. A light turned on at the end of the hallway, a door slammed, and then *clap, clap, clap* of hard-soled shoes. Someone was coming.

She quickly pulled her shoes off, then sprinted down the hallway, barefoot. Simon was saying something, but his words were garbled. She hesitated at the entranceway to the main exhibit area, which was empty.

She hurried through the main room, into the museum's entrance, out the door, into the night.

Chapter 12

Stakeout

Whitney leaned onto the dash of her rental car. Hugo was going to pay for the way he'd treated her. She'd seen the black Uber idling in front of the museum and figured it was Ellie's.

"There she is," Whitney said softly.

She watched Ellie close the museum door behind her. Her shoes dangled from her hand, and her purse hung from her shoulder, glittering from the outside lights. She hurried down the steps of the museum and then disappeared into the waiting car.

Why isn't she wearing her shoes? Whitney wondered.

Whitney gazed back to the museum door, expecting any second to see Hugo. Instead, the Lincoln Navigator's taillights flashed, and the car pulled away from the curb. *So, she's leaving alone.* Whitney tapped her fingers on the dash. *Maybe Hugo's just being careful.* She pulled her seat belt across her chest. *There's only one way to make sure,* she decided: follow Ellie home and wait.

Whitney crouched down in her seat as the Uber passed by, and then started her car. She cautiously pulled onto the road behind the Lincoln Navigator. Without using her blinker, she merged onto the highway, keeping far enough back to not raise suspicion.

Twenty minutes later, the car swerved onto a paved circular drive in front of a white and gray, shingled Cape Cod. Whitney drove past the house and looped around the block, coming to a stop a few houses away. She flicked off her headlights and ignition.

From her vantage point, she watched as the driver leaped from the SUV and opened the door for Olivia. Michael opened the door for Ellie on the other side. Anger instantly surged through Whitney's veins at the sight of Ellie.

Michael hugged both women and then stood watching until they disappeared into their house. The lights flickered on in the living room. Olivia leaned toward the window, waved goodbye to Michael, and then closed the curtains.

Michael climbed into the front passenger seat. The vehicle rumbled to life, eased out onto the road, and drove away.

Whitney looked around uneasily; the last thing she needed was a nosy neighbor calling the cops on her. Headlights shone in her rear window as a car approached. Whitney slid down into her seat until her eyes were just above the dash. The car slowed in front of Ellie's house. Whitney leaned forward onto the dash of her car.

A man exited the car, glanced toward Whitney's vehicle, and then made his way across the street. It wasn't Hugo; it was Ellie's neighbor. Whitney calmed herself and stretched her shoulders. *What if Hugo is already back at the hotel waiting for me? What would I tell him? He'd be worried to death. How has everything gotten to this point?* She remembered meeting Hugo after grad school, their first archeological dig together. She'd been mesmerized by every aspect of this man. A bitter taste filled her mouth. Sure, she'd been hypnotized by his charm, his charisma, but so had every woman who'd crossed paths with him. And now, here she was, protecting what was hers from yet another woman.

Whitney breathed in deeply, trying to clear the cobwebs that had filled her brain. Various lights flickered on and off in Ellie's house, and then all was dark except for the porchlight. Whitney was exhausted. Ellie and Olivia had obviously gone to bed like she should have done an hour ago. She started her rental, punched *Recent* on her GPS, selected the street address, and began the long drive back to her hotel.

Chapter 13

Fired

Rental cars and news vans with their clusters of antennae and satellite dishes lined the street beside the Bitter Sweet Café.

Michael eased up to the entrance of the parking lot, giving it a quick scan. Every space was filled. He continued past the café, took a left onto Atlantic, and pulled into the Lana Cove Seaside Park. It was another beautiful day. The wind blew across the ocean, waves crashed onto the shore, and a flock of seagulls, wings outstretched, navigated the wind currents, crying out in delight. A brooding pelican sat watching for fish atop a gray wooden post, a remnant from a pier washed away by Hurricane Hazel.

Michael grabbed his notepad and locked it in his trunk. There was no way he'd be able to write today; the café was too busy. *I'll just grab a coffee and bagel, say hi to the girls, and then write from home,* Michael thought.

He checked both ways and jogged across Atlantic Avenue. He stopped at the curb, allowing an elderly couple to pass by on their bicycles, before stepping onto the sidewalk. Michael was accosted by a cacophony of sound as he entered the café. The usually calm atmosphere was replaced by utter chaos. A line of hungry customers started at the counter and wrapped along the wall to the back of the restaurant.

Ellie worked the counter. Thick strands of hair had escaped her loose pony and hung in tendrils across her face. Olivia was red-faced, manning the cappuccino machine and filling orders.

"Sorry, gentlemen," Michael said, squeezing between a couple of men in black knit shirts, WRVA logos on their sleeves. "I work here," Michael lied, making his way to the front counter.

Ellie half-smiled, giving him a not-now look.

"I'm here to help," Michael explained. "Just tell me what to do."

Relief flooded Ellie's face. "How good are you at busing tables?" she asked frantically.

"The best!" Michael insisted.

"Wonderful. Ollie's the only busboy we've got right now."

"Great. I know Ollie." Michael nodded. "I'll find him and start bussing." He gave Ellie a smile and then made his way through the crowd, looking for Ollie, a freckled-faced, red-haired old soul who looked like the male version of Annie.

Michael found Ollie in the kitchen, emptying out a large gray plastic tub. "Hey, Ollie, I'm here to help you guys out. Ellie asked if I can bus tables. I told her of course, so here I am. Just tell me what to do."

"You're officially my best friend." Ollie smiled. "Here." He tossed Michael a crisp white apron and handed him a gray plastic tub. "There's only one important rule—"

"Don't get handsy with the ladies?"

"Okay," Ollie laughed, "two important rules. Just make sure that you ask before you take. I learned the hard way that what may look like trash isn't always trash."

"One man's crumbs are another man's muffin," Michael offered.

"Something like that." Ollie grinned. "Okay, silverware goes here." He pointed to a large bin in an industrial-sized washer. "Plates and cups here."

"Got it." Michael nodded, eyeing the stack of unwashed dishes. "I didn't see Jeff—is he working today?"

Ollie hesitated. "It's his sister's birthday. He never works on her birthday. We're really backed up, Michael." Ollie stopped him before he could ask another question. "I'll take the deck; you take the main dining area. If you have any questions, you know where to find me."

"Fair enough," Michael agreed.

"Good luck," Ollie called out as he exited the kitchen into the café.

Michael tied the apron around his waist, adjusted it, and set to work, clearing off tables, wiping down seats, answering questions, scuttling back and forth with armloads of dirty dishes. Clean, load up, empty his tub, scrape food into the trash, repeat. He wished he was wearing his Fitbit because he would be killing it right now.

"Well, well, well…."

Michael groaned. He knew that raspy voice. It belonged to Arthur Wisely, his octogenarian nemesis. "Good morning, Arthur. Isn't it a little early for you to be out of your coffin?"

"Tsk. Tsk. Insulting your elders," he said, shaking his head, "and in a skirt nonetheless." He pulled at the back of Michael's apron, untying his knot. The apron fell to the floor, puddling at his feet. "Oops." Arthur laughed mischievously, holding his hand to his face. "I guess that book deal fell through. Such a shame. I was looking forward to using it as toilet paper."

"Sorry to disappoint you, Arthur." Michael retied his apron. "I'm just helping Ellie and Olivia. They're a bit understaffed, as you can see." He gestured to the crowd. "And my book, by the way, is still on the path to greatness."

"Sure." Arthur laughed. "You keep telling yourself that. We've all got eyes, Michael; we know what's going on."

Mary Taylor nodded smugly, agreeing with Arthur.

"Sad, really. That handsome Hugo fella comes to town, steals Ellie and your manhood," Arthur said.

"That's why he's wearing the skirt," Mary whispered.

"It's an apron," Michael insisted and smoothed it out over his pants.

Arthur guffawed and blew out a mix of air and spittle.

Michael was just thankful his dentures didn't fly out as well.

"Maybe you should cut back on the coffee. Maybe decaf? A soy latte?" Michael offered.

"Look around you, Michael. All of these people with their fancy cameras and news trucks are here to see *Hugo*." He poked Michael in the chest with his gnarled finger. "*This* is what success feels like."

"And this is what a wet diaper feels like." Michael aimed the spray bottle at Arthur's crotch and gave him a few spritzes. "Look, everyone, Arthur wet himself."

"Well played, Mr. West," Arthur declared, grabbing a stack of napkins from the dispenser. "Well played, but now—you're fired."

"I don't work here." Michael winked. "You can't fire free help." He laughed and swiped Arthur's croissant, taking a bite. "This is really good."

"Hey!" Arthur cried out.

"Just looking out for your health, Arthur. These things are *loaded* with sugar and butter. Plus…." He stuffed the rest into his mouth. "I haven't had breakfast."

"This isn't over." Arthur shook his fist.

"I love you, too," Michael said over his shoulder. "Enjoy your breakfast."

Michael's shoulders ached. He slowly rotated them and tilted his head from side to side. He couldn't remember the last time he'd worked so hard. He leaned over the sink and washed his hands and forearms. They were covered in dried syrup, coffee, and grime.

"Mr. West," a woman's voice rang out behind him. "We had a customer complaint about you today."

A smile spread across Michael's face as he finished washing his hands. "Just one?" he asked innocently.

"We take these complaints very seriously. A gentleman by the name of Arthur Wisely said, and I quote, 'Michael harassed me and then accosted me with a spray bottle.'"

Michael snatched a paper towel from the dispenser above the sink. "I'm guilty. I sprayed with malicious intent." He shook his head slowly. "I guess this means...."

"You're fired," Olivia said, giving him a hug. "We're going to have to let you go."

"Seems like you're doing just the opposite," Michael pointed out.

"Ah, clever!" Olivia laughed.

"What's going on back here?" Ellie pushed through the hanging doorway into the back room.

"I was just firing Mr. West for his egregious act."

"Arthur could use a little humility every now and then." Ellie laughed. She gave Michael a huge hug. "Thank you so much for stepping in today and helping. It was insane. I talked to reporters from France, Germany, India—well, from all over the world."

Olivia looked at her watch. "It's three o'clock. We're supposed to be at the museum at six-thirty."

She looked around the filthy kitchen. "Not sure how we're going to—"

"I'll help," Michael insisted, "just let me know what needs to be done. Oh, wait…I forgot, I'm fired."

Ellie smiled at Olivia and motioned her over. "Just a moment, Mr. West."

The two friends whispered for a few seconds and then turned to Michael.

"We've decided that you've learned a valuable lesson. You are reinstated. So, consider this your first and last warning," Ellie said.

"Yes." Olivia nodded. "You're officially un-fired, but if you step out of line again…let's just say things aren't going to end well."

Chapter 14

Blazing News

Ellie, Olivia, and Michael stood on the steps of the museum in the sweltering summer heat. Ellie had insisted that they arrive an hour early. Now, Michael was sure she regretted it. She and Olivia fanned themselves with their hands, their cheeks flushed red. He removed his black sport coat and folded it over his arm.

The doorman from the night before opened the door and stepped onto the landing. Cool air swirled around him. "Elite VIPs," he called out, "we will be ushering you into the museum in five minutes. Please make sure you have your passes available."

He moved aside as two shirtless pharaohs, wearing traditional Egyptian headdresses, walked along the long line of overheated guests, passing out ice-cold Perrier. Michael thanked the man and held the glass bottle against his forehead.

A red carpet extended from the doorway to the street. The line of guests stretched down the sidewalk for another fifty feet.

"You know," Michael said, twisting the cap off his Perrier. "I don't recall seeing Hugo at the café today."

"Me neither." Olivia took a sip from her bottle.

"He's probably getting ready for the event," Ellie reasoned. "I'm sure he had a lot to do."

"At least this time he's actually opening the sarcophagus. Not much could go wrong there, except for dull scissors, or whatever they use to cut those seals."

"I wonder if that angry reporter, Ivan, is going to make an appearance." Olivia said.

"Doubt it," Michael presumed.

"You guys didn't hear?" asked a woman's voice.

The trio turned in unison. A pale, squat woman in a sparkly, long-sleeved black dress stood on the step below them. She looked miserable in the abominable heat.

"I'm sorry, I wasn't trying to eavesdrop. It's just that we're in such close proximity." She blinked constantly from the sweat pouring down her brow.

"Not a problem," Michael said kindly. He pulled a handkerchief from his jacket pocket. "Here you go.

I promise it's unused." He winked. "Were you here last night?"

"Thank you. Yes, it's the reason I wore this." She gestured to her outfit. "I nearly froze from the air-conditioning last night, so I decided to wear something a little warmer. I didn't realize I'd be participating in a reenactment of *Dante's Inferno*."

"That's funny." Olivia laughed. "It was a bit chilly. You were about to say something about Ivan, the reporter?"

"Yes, he wrote a nasty article about Hugo last night, calling him a con artist, bilking the public and twisting history with his stories about Baal and equating his importance to that of Tutankhamen. He also published a heavily edited video from last night that made Hugo look like a raging lunatic."

Michael nodded. "After last night's events, I'm sure it didn't require too much editing. Hugo did go after him pretty hard."

"Only after Ivan attacked him," Ellie added a little too defensively.

"Yes, but Hugo could have defused things…instead, he decided to turn their argument into a social experiment at Ivan's expense."

"The story is already gaining traction. As of this afternoon, it had already been viewed over 150,000 times, and several news groups have already picked it up." The woman pointed beyond Ellie's shoulder. "They're opening the doors."

Theodopolus pushed past the startled doorman and grabbed Ellie's wrist. "Come with me." Theodopolus seemed flustered, angry. "Frederick," he said sternly, "let them in." He pointed to Olivia and Michael, who were trying to get inside. "They're with me."

Frederick the doorman stepped aside, allowing Michael and Olivia to follow.

"What's going on?" demanded Michael as he straightened his suit jacket. "Since when did museums need a bouncer?"

Theodopolus ignored Michael's questions and turned to a security guard. "Peyton, secure three seats in front of the sarcophagus for them. You three, follow me."

Chapter 15

Accused

"Mr. Withers," Ellie demanded, "I think we need an explanation."

He glanced at Ellie over his shoulder. His jaw muscles flexed. "This way," he said sharply, directing them into the same hallway that led to the room where Ellie had left her purse.

Her heart began to beat quickly. *Was this about her sneaking back into the museum? Did they have her on camera eavesdropping?* As she turned and looked over her shoulder, a security camera stared back at her, its red light flashing.

"Mr. Withers," Ellie began, attempting to explain why she had been there last night. "I think this is all a big mistake."

"What do you mean, Miss Banks, by a big mistake?" Theodopolus asked coming to an abrupt stop inside the administrative hallway. "Have you seen Hugo?"

"What?" Ellie was thrown by the question. "What do you mean?"

"Precisely what I asked," he replied bluntly. "Have you seen him?"

"Not since last night. He didn't come to the café this morning, if that's what you're asking," Ellie replied, an edge to her voice.

"When was the last time you saw him?"

Why was he asking these questions? Ellie thought for a moment. Should she say anything about overhearing his conversation? "The last time I saw him was with you, in your office to get the VIP passes—and then he walked me back to the main hall. Mr. Withers, I'm not saying another word until you tell me why you're asking me all these questions."

Theodopolus simply stared back at her. "He's missing, Ellie. No one has seen him since last night."

"Missing…?" Ellie asked, her eyes wide.

"There she is!" Whitney's voice rang out. Everyone's heads turned as Whitney stormed down the hallway, Oscar and Simon close on her heels.

"Where is Hugo?" Whitney demanded, pushing past Theodopolus, grabbing Ellie by the shoulders. "What did you do to Hugo?"

Ellie shrugged Whitney's hands off her shoulders. "I don't know what you're talking about! I don't know what any of this is about!" she said angrily.

"All I know is Hugo invited us to the grand opening. We show up and then we're suddenly interrogated as if we're criminals."

"If you're implying that something happened to Hugo and that Ellie had something to do with it, you're dead wrong," Olivia said furiously. "And," she added, addressing both Whitney and Theodopolus, "you both owe her an apology."

"You're right, you're right," Theodopolus insisted. "I'm acting like a fool. The truth of the matter is, no one has seen Hugo since last night, and we have a sold-out event. And after last night's fiasco, we really needed a win."

"Ellie left here and went straight home," Olivia said sharply, in defense of her friend. "No one else came to our house last night if that is what you were trying to imply." Olivia stared down Whitney and Theodopolus.

"Well, Hugo never showed up at the hotel, so he had to have been somewhere. He's not answering his phone, his texts…," Whitney had lost the fire in her voice. She looked like she was about to break down. "Simon said he left just a few minutes after I did," she said softly.

Simon nodded in agreement. Ellie wondered if Simon had told Whitney that he and Hugo had been arguing.

"Look," Oscar said, exasperated. "Who *knows* where Hugo is? The man has issues with responsibility, okay. He's probably drunk somewhere, with some floozy."

Simon grabbed the front of Oscar's shirt and drew up his fist. "Hugo's my friend—don't you talk about him that way."

"You better think twice about what you're doing," Oscar sneered. "I'll ruin your life."

Simon stared at Oscar, and after a few tense moments, he released his shirt and dropped his hand to his side. Everyone knew what he was thinking, and it wasn't pleasant.

"That's better." Oscar smiled smugly as he straightened his shirt. "Now, I've invested over a hundred thousand on this little Egyptian foray. If Hugo is a no-show—"

"I'll do the show," Simon interrupted.

Everyone turned to him. "I can run the show." Simon looked horrible. His exuberance was belied by the puffy dark crescents beneath his eyes.

"You can't even operate simple machinery," Oscar sneered, "and you think I'm going to let you—"

"Oscar...," Theodopolus interrupted, putting his hand on his shoulder. "Everyone's on edge. Nothing is going right. But we can't all turn on each other like a pack of wolves." He turned his attention to Simon. "Hugo's not here—can you really do this?"

"I've helped Hugo launch hundreds of exhibits throughout the world," explained Simon. "I can do this."

Theodopolus met his eyes and nodded. "All right, Simon, go get ready. Ellie." He adjusted his wire-framed glasses. "Ellie's friends." He smiled. "My humblest apologies. I'm so incredibly sorry for my behavior."

"Mr. Withers," Ellie spoke kindly, "I can understand. It's been one thing after another. The stress, I'm sure, is horrible."

"Thank you for understanding." He smiled compassionately. "If you would allow me." He held out his arm to her. "May I escort you to your seat?"

"Thank you." Ellie smiled.

"Once again, you're stuck with me." Michael grinned, holding out his arm to Olivia.

Chapter 16

The Show Must Go On

Michael sat in the front row, facing the sarcophagus, Ellie and Olivia on either side of him. They had been ushered to their seats ahead of the VIP ticket holders.

"I'm going to take some pictures before the crowds arrive," Michael said. He slid from his seat and crouched in front of the velvet rope that encircled the sarcophagus. He zoomed and began taking a series of pictures of the intricately designed patterns painted on the top and side of the coffin.

Excited voices echoed in the hallway; the museum doors had been opened for the elite VIP guests. Michael switched his phone to video mode and hurriedly maneuvered around the sarcophagus. He'd just finished circling when the crowd of enthusiastic VIPs surrounded him. He moved out of the way so they could photograph and video Baal's wooden coffin.

"I got some great shots. I'll send you guys copies," he said when he returned to his seat.

"Thanks," Ellie replied, torn between the excitement and the mystery behind Hugo's strange disappearance.

Simon proved to be just as talented as Hugo when it came to showmanship. By the time he and the Egyptian dignitaries removed the seals and opened the sarcophagus, he had everyone on the edge of their seats.

He allowed groups of four to view Baal. His withered face was uncovered, and a linen cloth covered in ancient hieroglyphics lay over his eyes. His mouth was open, revealing his upper gum. A cluster of yellow broken teeth remained. His body was wrapped in linen, much of which had deteriorated and taken on a brownish-red hue.

When it was their turn, Michael, Ellie, and Olivia approached the sarcophagus reverently. It seemed surreal to be gazing down upon a historical figure, buried for thousands of years.

"Simon, what are the hieroglyphics written on his wrappings?" Olivia asked.

"Those are spells written during the mummification process. They serve two purposes. The first is to reunite the soul and the body in the afterlife and the second is to help guide him along his journey in his afterlife. The papyrus scrolls in the display…," he gestured to a glass enclosure, "…are what the Egyptians called the Book of the Dead."

"Book of the Dead sounds a little creepy," Ellie smiled.

"You must remember the Egyptians looked at death differently. Death was a magical journey that led to a place where there was no pain or suffering. However, the journey was complex. The Book of the Dead was filled with incantations and spells that they needed to use in the right sequence to proceed into the afterlife."

"Simon, please don't think that I'm being disrespectful, but doesn't this disprove Egyptian magic and their idea of life after death?" Michael asked.

"What do you mean?" Simon's voice carried a hint of annoyance.

"You said that the hieroglyphics written on the linen and the Book of the Dead were written to help reunite the body and the spirit, so they could use their bodies in the afterlife."

"Correct," Simon answered slowly.

"And yet his body is still here, as are Tutankhamun's and hundreds of others, so if they are here, how are they supposed to use them in the afterlife?"

Simon smiled. "That's a great question, Michael. Just like Christianity, or most modern-day religions, there is a promised afterlife where we imagine we will be just as we are now, except we'll be living for all eternity, seeing our families and friends again. Yet their bodies remain here on Earth. No one truly knows. Whether you believe in magic or your deity, both require faith. Perhaps the reunification of the mummy's soul and body takes thousands of years, a mere blink in the hands of time. But the truth is, no one truly knows, and for now, maybe as Baal slumbers beneath his wrappings, his spirit is watching us all, judging us by our very deeds."

"Something to think about," Michael replied.

"Thanks a lot," Olivia whispered, smacking Michael's shoulder. "Now you've got Baal's spirit angry at us. I probably won't be able to sleep tonight."

"She's right," Simon smiled. "Be careful of the ill you speak, upon your life misfortune wreaks."

"And you're cursed," Olivia exclaimed. "Come on, Michael, back to your seat."

"It rhymes, so it must be true," Michael teased.

"You just told history's most evil sorcerer that he's not going to go to his afterlife, but he will be going on a world tour, to be gawked at by thousands of people."

"I'm sure he'll be okay with it. And," he said, holding up his phone, "I got some great pictures and videos to remind me of this magical moment."

"Great." Olivia smirked. "Maybe he can track you that way."

Ellie rolled her eyes. "You can dress them up, but you can't take them anywhere."

Chapter 17

Reconciled

"I don't get it," Ellie said, as they walked through the museum parking lot. "Hugo lives for the spotlight—he loves attention. And here we are...," she gestured to the news vans, the main event, "...and he's a no-show." She pressed the remote to unlock her silver Acura.

"Maybe his amulet didn't work," Michael joked, not terribly upset that Hugo was absent. "Didn't Oscar say he had commitment issues?"

Olivia nudged Michael's shoulder. "Keep it down," she whispered.

She tilted her head toward Whitney, who was leaning against the trunk of her burgundy rental car, cradling her cell phone between her shoulder and cheek. Her head was tilted down—tears streamed down her face.

Whitney looked up, recognizing Ellie as they approached her car.

Oh great…. Ellie braced herself for another tirade. She rethought her initial response when she saw Whitney's makeup-streaked face, red and swollen. "Whitney, are you okay?"

Whitney inhaled and pulled her shoulders back, attempting to put on a brave face, but she broke down sobbing again. She sniffled and wiped her nose on her sleeve.

Michael reached for his handkerchief, then remembered he'd given it to the woman on the steps.

"One second." Ellie rushed around her car to the passenger's side. She leaned in, popped open the glovebox, and grabbed a couple of tissues. "Here." She handed them to Whitney. "Extra soft with aloe." She smiled.

"Thank you." Whitney dabbed her nose and straightened her dress. "Ellie, I'm not going to be angry with you, no matter what you tell me. I just need to know…." She closed her eyes and took a deep breath; her entire body shuddered. "Did you see Hugo last night?" she blurted out. "I just need to know that he's okay." Her voice grew smaller as if she were shrinking.

Ellie shook her head. "I'm sorry, Whitney, the last time I saw him was at the event. I figured he'd left and met you at the hotel."

"No," Whitney said quietly.

"Has he ever done this before?" Olivia asked, her voice soft.

Whitney wiped her eyes with the back of her hands, smudging her makeup, creating dark blue streaks across her cheeks. "Hugo's always been a big flirt. To him, it's all a big game. He knows that I know…and he knows not to push things too far." Whitney's voice caught in her throat. "But he always comes back."

"Has he ever missed an event, a grand opening?" Olivia asked gently.

"Never," Whitney declared as if the thought of such a thing were ludicrous. "I've known him for four years. He's never missed an opening. There's too much money at stake. No, something has happened."

Ellie thought for a moment and then decided to confess what she'd heard inside the museum when she'd gone back to get her purse. "Whitney, I was telling the truth when I said the last time I saw Hugo was at the event. However, that's not everything…."

Whitney stared at Ellie. She was listening so intently, it was as if she'd stopped breathing. "Go on," she whispered.

"Remember when I came back to the museum, I told you I left my purse inside?"

Whitney nodded. "Was that a lie? Were you trying to meet Hugo?"

"No, I really did leave my purse in one of the administrative offices. However, when I was leaving, I heard Hugo screaming at Simon." Ellie felt her face go red as she admitted to eavesdropping. "I know I shouldn't have, but I lingered in the hallway. My curiosity won over my reasoning."

"What were they arguing about?" Whitney asked.

"Something about CT scans or x-rays of the mummy. Hugo was insisting that Simon had taken scans of the mummy, and Simon was saying that he'd only taken calibration images. Simon said that the only pictures that he had were the portable x-ray scans taken in Egypt."

"That doesn't make sense," Whitney said. "I saw Simon taking scans of Baal to test the equipment that morning."

"Did you see the images?" Michael asked.

"No, Simon kicked me out of the room. He said I needed a radiation vest, and that he only had one."

"How convenient," Michael muttered.

"Did you hear anything else?" Whitney asked.

Ellie thought back to the conversation. She replayed the conversation in her mind. "I didn't hear much more. The argument seemed to wind down, and then I heard someone coming down the hall...." Ellie's face went red again. "...So, I ran. After that, we left and went home."

Michael and Olivia nodded, confirming Ellie's story.

"Does Simon have any ideas?" Olivia asked.

"No." Whitney shook her head. "Simon said that he and Hugo stayed for a while to discuss the grand opening. They had a drink together, and then Hugo got an Uber and took off."

"Did Simon see him get in the Uber," Michael asked, "or did he just see him getting a driver through the app?"

"He didn't say."

"Well, that's where I would start," Michael suggested. "Find out who picked him up and where they took him."

"Simon's worried that the journalist that Hugo insulted came after him. He wrote an article saying Hugo is a fraud and thrives on greed and deception...."

"A woman in line told us about Ivan's article and video," Ellie acknowledged.

Michael shook his head. "Guys, Ivan weighs 120 pounds soaking wet. He's the kind of guy who fights from afar, hidden behind a keyboard. He's not one for a physical altercation."

"So, you don't think he's a threat?"

"Maybe a threat to Hugo's reputation. But physically...." He let his words hang in the air.

"I just don't see anything happening to him here in Lana Cove. The most dangerous group we have here is the beachcombers," Olivia offered.

"Who are they, a gang?" Whitney asked, surprised.

"Yes." Michael nodded sagely. "They're a group of angry octogenarians wielding metal detectors and plastic shovels. You encroach on their turf, and it's lights out." He punched his fist into the palm of his hand.

Ellie rolled her eyes. "Sorry, Michael has a bit of an overactive imagination."

"What?" he asked, defensively. "How about Matt Williams?"

"What about Matt Williams?" Ellie countered. "He was at the café today enjoying a bagel and a caramel macchiato."

"The beachcombers crept into his yard, under the shadows of darkness, turned on his garden hose, and flooded his award-winning petunias. Not a single flower was able to be saved." He turned to Whitney, his face serious. "They are not to be underestimated," he declared. "They move with the stealth of ninjas." He moved his hands across his body and assumed a martial arts pose.

"Dear God," Whitney whispered.

"Don't listen to him, he's an idiot." Ellie smacked Michael on the back of the head.

"My uncle is a detective for the Lana Cove Police Department. I'll give him a call and see if he's heard anything. If you'd like, I can go to the police station with you and file a missing person report," Olivia offered.

"Don't we have to wait twenty-four hours?" Whitney asked.

"No. It's better if we get the ball rolling now. There are only two hospitals in Lana Cove—we can call and check with them as well," Olivia suggested.

"Okay." Whitney nodded. "I'd appreciate that."

"Not a problem." Olivia stepped away from the group to make the call.

"You guys are so incredibly nice. I'm ashamed that I acted so rudely."

"Water under the bridge," Ellie reassured her. She placed her hand on Whitney's shoulder. "Don't worry, we'll get to the bottom of this."

Whitney fought back her tears and tried to smile. "I know," she said softly.

Moments later, Olivia rejoined the group. "He said that only two reports were filed last night—"

"Was there another attack by the beachcombers?" Michael interrupted.

"You," Ellie pointed, "go wait in the car."

"One was a man complaining of chest pains, but he doesn't fit Hugo's description. The other was a noise violation. He wants us to run by the station and fill out a missing person report. Is that all right with you, Whitney?"

"Yes, of course, anything they need," she replied.

"Ellie." Olivia turned to her friend. "You look utterly exhausted."

"I'm okay," Ellie insisted, waving away Olivia's comment.

"Michael, why don't you give Ellie a lift home, and if it's okay with you," she turned back to Whitney, "I'll ride to the police station with you."

Whitney nodded her agreement. "That would be nice, thank you."

"I can run back to the station and get you once you're finished," Michael offered.

"No, get some rest. My uncle or one of the other officers can give me a ride home afterward. Not like they've got anything else to do." Olivia smiled.

Ellie was about to object, but she knew Olivia was right, plus, she had to open the café at five in the morning. "Okay," Ellie agreed, hugging her friend. "Be safe." She turned to Whitney. "Everything will work out," she said and hugged her, too.

Chapter 18

Too Many Questions

"Good morning, Olivia. Detective Adams, aren't you looking spiffy."

"Morning, Michael," he said, blowing across the top of his coffee.

"Mind if I join you?" Michael asked.

Detective Adams ran his hair through his salt-and-pepper hair and let out an annoyed sigh.

"Not at all," Olivia insisted. "We're waiting for Ellie. Uncle Louie wants to ask her a few questions."

"Do you mind if I call you Uncle Louie, too?" Michael asked Detective Adams, as he slid his chair beneath the table.

Detective Adams tilted his head toward Michael, and raised his eyebrows, giving him a have-you-lost-your-mind look.

"I'm gonna say that's a no. Any news on Hugo's whereabouts?" Michael inquired to change gears.

"Nothing yet," Detective Adams replied. "I'm still creating a timeline. I've got a few missing pieces that need to find a home."

"I was just studying about the importance of establishing a timeline in an investigation. It's quite fascinating."

"Really?" Detective Adams took a bite of his cream cheese bagel and wiped the corners of his mouth with his napkin. "What, are you binge-watching *Murder, She Wrote*?"

"Michael's studying to be a private investigator," Olivia interjected excitedly before Michael had a chance to respond.

"Heaven help us." Detective Adams sighed. "Michael, not to be rude, but you're not really private eye material. Wasn't having your thumb broken and getting shot enough for you?"

"Yes, I certainly don't care to relive either of those moments. And before you give yourself an ulcer, I'm just taking an online certification course and working with Steele Investigative Group to help add some authenticity to my books."

Relief passed across Detective Adams's face. "Well, that's quite noble of you. In reality, police work isn't glamourous; it's the dogged pursuit of truth through painstaking research."

"I know, I've been on the receiving end of one of your investigations. Not one of my fondest memories."

Michael's comment got an unexpected snort out of the detective.

"So…." Michael clasped his hands together, eager to move the conversation away from him. "What have you discovered so far? Were you able to question Simon?"

"I was. Detective Mitchell and I got a brief statement from him this morning. Not the best interview, but I think we got what we needed."

Olivia looked at him curiously. "Was there a problem?"

"Simon was a bit preoccupied with a CNN interview," Detective Adams explained. "We got there about ten minutes before they arrived. Needless to say, he wasn't very focused."

"It's not looking good for Hugo, is it?"

Detective Adams hesitated for a moment and then shook his head. "No, it's not."

"Did Simon offer any explanation?"

"He said he's known Hugo for years, and that he's never missed an opening. This was a significant find; Hugo wouldn't have missed it."

"Did Simon mention that he had an argument with Hugo?"

Detective Adams arched his eyebrows as if surprised by the question. "Yes, why?"

"I wonder if what he told you and what Ellie heard match up," Michael pondered aloud.

Detective Adams rested his hands on the table. He gave Michael his full attention; his face became serious. "What did Ellie hear?"

"Ellie, Olivia, and I were leaving the museum. We'd just pulled out of the parking lot when Ellie realized she'd left her purse inside the museum."

"What time was this?"

"I think it was about ten o'clock." Michael glanced at Olivia, looking for confirmation. She nodded in agreement.

"We returned to the museum and Ellie ran inside. She said she'd heard Hugo and Simon arguing about pictures."

Detective Adams slipped his hand inside his sport coat and removed a black, leather-bound notebook.

"What pictures?"

"Pictures of the mummy. Simon said that he didn't take any pictures of the mummy; he only took…." Michael snapped his fingers, trying to remember the terminology.

"Calibration scans," Olivia helped, "not actual pictures."

"Thank you, Olivia." Michael smiled.

"I do everything I can to help the elderly." She beamed.

"Why would they get in a fight over pictures? Seems inconsequential in the grand scheme of things," Detective Adams asked.

"I'm not sure," Michael said. "Hugo had a rough night. He was humiliated in front of everyone. Maybe he just picked out something to use as a catalyst for an argument."

"Maybe." Detective Adams tapped his mechanical pencil on the tabletop as he read through his notes.

"Does that match his statement?" Michael asked.

"It does, except there's no mention of pictures in his statement."

"Like you said, probably inconsequential. So, he forgot about it. Ellie returned to the car, and we left and went home."

"Simon told me that the argument was about a piece of equipment not working. He said there was a software update in the middle of the presentation, and it basically ruined the exhibit."

Michael nodded. "That's correct. They wheeled out this giant CT scanner, and they were supposed to push the sarcophagus through it so we could see inside."

"Was there a reason why they couldn't open it?"

"Yes, dignitaries from Egypt were attending the grand opening the next night. The sarcophagus was sealed, and Hugo was going to cut the seals in the presence of the dignitaries."

Detective Adams nodded, jotting notes into his pad.

"So," Michael continued, "just as they're about to scan the sarcophagus, the machine says it needs a software update. Then when Hugo found out that the update could take as long as two hours; he lost his cool."

"I see." Detective Adams scribbled in his notebook.

"The night pretty much broke up after that. Hugo apologized for the inconvenience and invited everyone there to come to the event the next night."

"And Ellie returned to the museum, after the event was over, to retrieve her purse, and that's when she heard Hugo and Simon arguing?"

"Correct." Michael nodded. "Detective Adams, did Simon say anything about seeing Hugo leave?"

"Simon said Hugo was exhausted and wanted to get back to the hotel. He said he saw him schedule an Uber on his phone, and that he left shortly thereafter. The security guard confirmed seeing Hugo leave."

"Were they all staying at the same hotel?" Olivia asked.

"Yes," Detective Adams confirmed, "everyone was staying at the Bay Breeze Hotel. Whitney and Hugo were sharing a room, and Simon was a few doors down."

"So, Hugo leaves the museum, the guard sees him leave, he gets into an Uber and then vanishes. Did the guard see him get into a car?"

"That's a good question, Michael, but without a good answer. He saw him exit the museum, but he never saw him get into a vehicle."

"Shouldn't Uber be able to provide that information?" Olivia asked. "And, don't they have surveillance cameras mounted outside?"

"Detective Mitchell has a call in to Uber. They'll be able to provide us with the driver and where he took Hugo. As far as cameras are concerned, we've requested access to their digital archives. Our tech guy is going to scrub those and let us know what he finds."

"So, Hugo leaves. Who else is left at the museum? Simon, the guard...anyone else?" Michael asked.

"Theodopolus Withers was still there. He was in his office following up on emails and voicemails. According to him, he and Simon left together about thirty minutes after Hugo departed."

"I'm guessing they didn't see anything suspicious?"

"Neither one said they saw anything. Theodopolus's car was in his designated parking spot, and he said Simon got into a black Prius. Theodopolus said Simon pulled out ahead of him and headed north, and he went directly home. Simon's story matches Theo's, except he stopped for gas at the Chevron station on Bending Tree Road, and then drove straight to the hotel and went to bed. Both men's testimony was corroborated by Peyton Leek, the museum guard."

"So, whatever happened to Hugo happened after he left the museum," Olivia surmised.

"It certainly appears that way," Detective Adams agreed. He looked up as Ellie approached the table, a pot of coffee in her hand. "Ellie," he said, jumping to his feet and kissing her on the cheek, "you read my mind."

Michael slid his chair from beneath the table and gave Ellie a hug. He could see from the dark circles beneath her eyes that she was still exhausted. "Want me to pitch in and give you guys a hand this morning? I see there's still a lot of news crews and tourists here."

Ellie's cheeks reddened as she took a seat at the table. "That would be wonderful, Michael—thank you so much."

"Not a problem at all. It's a nice change of pace."

"I'd planned for a couple days of larger crowds," Ellie exclaimed, "but with Hugo missing, that's become their biggest news story. I overheard table three over there putting together a story called *The Curse of Baal*."

"You may have to deal with larger crowds for a while," Michael said as he looked out over the crowded café. "I'll help out as much as I can till things calm down."

"Careful what you say, Michael," Olivia laughed, "we may never let you leave." She stood and hugged her uncle once more, and then disappeared behind the counter.

"Louie," Ellie said, "I'm so sorry to keep you waiting. I've got about ten minutes, then I've got to get back to work."

"Of course. Thank you for squeezing me in, Ellie." Detective Adams emptied a packet of sugar into his coffee. "Michael was telling me that you went back into the museum to retrieve your purse."

"Yes, after the exhibit was over."

"What happened then?"

"I ran to the door, thinking it would be locked, when Whitney pushed it open. We had words."

Detective Adams looked up from his notebook. "Because you returned to the museum after hours?"

Ellie blushed from her cheeks to the tips of her ears. "You have to understand, Hugo is this larger-than-life character, and a humongous flirt. He gave us tickets to the premiere, and when I arrived, he made a big deal about me being there in front of the cameras. It really set Whitney off."

Ellie looked down at the table. "I guess I got a little caught up in everything and should have been a little more restrained, because I really upset Whitney."

"So, Whitney opened the door, she sees you, and she assumed that you returned to see Hugo?"

"Exactly. I tried to explain that I had left my purse, that there was nothing between me and Hugo, but of course she didn't believe me…and I don't blame her."

Detective Adams patted her hand and asked her gently to continue.

"Once inside I didn't see anyone, so I hurried through the museum to the administrative offices. I could hear Hugo yelling at Simon."

"What were they arguing about?"

"CT scans, pictures of the mummy. He told Simon that he knew he had scans of the mummy, but Simon told him he couldn't access the images while the software was updating."

"Oh, so he didn't deny taking the pictures?"

"Well, yes and no. He said he hadn't taken any other pictures, only calibration images. He also told Hugo that it was his idea not to store the files on the museum's computers for fear of someone hacking them and publishing them before the event."

Detective Adams was busy writing in his notebook.

"Oh, and I heard a crash. Like a mirror shattering or a glass breaking."

"When was this?"

"At the beginning of the conversation, when Hugo was screaming."

"So maybe someone threw a glass or something in anger."

"I'm only going by what I heard," Ellie replied.

"This is perfect, Ellie." Detective Adams smiled. "Then what happened?"

"Hugo stopped yelling. Simon began praising him, telling him that the software update was unpredictable, that Hugo had turned a disaster into a success. He said he had the journalists literally drooling over the opportunity to photograph and video Baal. He basically fed Hugo's ego."

Detective Adams looked up from his notepad. "Is there anything else you can remember?"

"Not really." Ellie shook her head. "I felt horrible for eavesdropping, so I kind of snuck through the museum and left as quietly as I could."

"Did you see anyone, hear anything when you left? Parking lot, street?" he added.

"No. Well, I saw a motorcycle buzz by as I climbed into the Uber with Michael and Olivia, but no, I didn't hear or see anything suspicious."

Detective Adams leaned back in his seat and stretched.

"If I may, I have a question. What about Ivan, the guy from the *New York Times*? I'd written him off as a self-righteous egotist." Michael shrugged. "But you never know. Was he questioned?"

"Interesting that you mentioned him." Detective Adams smiled. "He's got quite a powerful hate campaign running against Hugo. He's calling it *The Hugo Conspiracy*."

"Not very catchy," Michael stated.

"Social media is frightening. Hugo has one argument with this guy and he's on a mission to destroy him. He even offered to apologize to the man," Ellie exclaimed.

"He's quite the winner," Detective Adams agreed, "but there's a little more to his story."

Ellie stole a quick glance at the front counter. "Okay, but then I've got to run."

"I asked Simon if Hugo had any enemies. He said that there is a lot of rivalry and hostility, especially overseas. Huge archeological discoveries bring in a lot of money and create a lot of enemies."

"But Ivan hardly seems to fit in there. He's a *Washington Post* journalist, just working on a story," said Michael.

Detective Adams took a sip of water; a twinkle filled his eyes. "Ivan's real name is Milo Kaminski. He had secured an assignment with the *Washington Post* to travel to Egypt with Hugo's team to document their research. However, about two months before they departed, Milo was charged with drunk driving and hit-and-run. This was Milo's second offense for driving under the influence. According to his police report, Milo was put on probation for six months and fired from the *Washington Post*."

"So, how did he get his press pass to get into the museum?" Ellie asked.

"Most likely forged. Probably used his old credentials. When I spoke to Theodopolus, he said he could've probably done a better job checking backgrounds of attendees beforehand."

"That's comforting," Michael mumbled.

"Hugo drove the final nail into Milo's coffin when he had him removed from their expedition and replaced him with a freelance journalist, who wasn't tied to any particular news source."

"But why didn't Hugo recognize him, or had they never met?" Michael said, answering his own question.

"I don't believe they ever met. I believe their correspondence was through emails and phone calls. No one from Hugo's team recognized him."

"I'm taking it that you haven't spoken to him yet."

"Not yet. The DMV has a New York address for him. We're working with the local NYPD to track him down."

"You think he would be capable of murdering someone?" Ellie asked.

"Let's say he's an empty box I'd like ticked. Milo has a criminal past. The man is lucky he's not behind bars. After the crash, he left the driver of the other vehicle slumped unconscious over the steering wheel. Had it not been for his well-connected lawyer, Milo would be in jail right now. Do I think he is capable of killing someone?" Detective Adams steepled his fingers. "Yes."

Chapter 19

Brainstorming

"This is just what I needed." Olivia laid her head back on her chair and closed her eyes, feeling the warmth of the sunlight on her face. She stretched her legs out in front of her and wiggled her toes.

Ellie took a long sip of her Mai Tai. "It's been a rough couple of days, that's for sure." She inhaled the warm, salty, ocean air deep into her lungs.

The trio sat together at an old rickety picnic table, one of twenty that stretched out in rows along the Atlantic Coast pier. Built in the early '70s, the Atlantic Coast Restaurant was constructed on a massive wooden dock that stretched out some two hundred feet into the ocean. The restaurant proper and bar was housed inside a squat white building that sat at the entrance.

The décor was simple. Strands of colored lights and old fishing nets were attached to the railings, and at the back of the pier, a large plastic shark dangled from a scale so tourists could take pictures. Local fishermen stood along the railings, cutting their baitfish and casting their lines.

Michael leaned against the weatherworn barrier and looked down at the waves crashing against the pilings, making their white-capped journey to the shore. High above, a group of pelicans soared through the air, riding the air currents, wings outstretched like ancient pterodactyls.

A gust of wind swept across their table, and their red and white checkered tablecloth rippled and flapped.

"If the wind picks up anymore, we'll be able to ride this thing like a magic carpet," Michael commented.

"Agreed." Olivia smiled. "As long as we can take these delicious Mai Tais, I'm fine with that."

Ellie reached into the large basket of golden hushpuppies and held one aloft between her fingertips. "I'm not sure how something so small could taste so good."

"We always want the things that are bad for us," Olivia agreed. "Like forbidden fruit." She eyed Michael mischievously.

"Is there actually a forbidden fruit?" Michael inquired.

"Of course," Ellie remarked. "Everyone knows the story of Eve and the apple."

Michael waved the reference aside. "If you want to tempt me, you better have a forbidden donut or croissant. I'd have no problem turning down an apple, *especially* from a talking snake."

Ellie sat eyeing Michael, a playful grin on her face. "Michael West, if I had to describe you as a fruit, I would have to say you're an *olive*." She waited a beat and then added, "An acquired taste."

"Is an olive even a fruit?" Michael asked, doubting her comment.

"Google says yes," Olivia replied, returning her phone to the table.

"Well, I'm fine with that." He smiled. "I find olives to be sophisticated, charming, and unassuming."

"Sometimes you make zero sense…," Ellie shook her head. "But you are cheap labor, so I guess we'll keep you around. Right, Livs?"

Olivia held up a finger. She was staring at her phone. "Whitney just texted me."

"Whitney? She has your number?" Ellie looked surprised.

"Fraternizing with the enemy," Michael smiled, happily watching Ellie squirm.

"How did she get your phone number?" Ellie asked, regaining her composure.

"I gave it to her when we left the police station. I told her to text me if she needed me." Olivia slid her thumb down the screen, reading. "She said Simon just returned to the hotel in a new rental car." She turned her phone so Ellie and Michael could see the screen.

"That color does not suit him at all," Michael declared, shaking his head. "He's more of an autumn."

"Looks like she took it from her balcony," Ellie added.

"She must have been waiting for him, or just got lucky," Michael speculated.

"What should I reply? That's one *yellow* car," Olivia proposed.

"Ask her why she thinks Simon got a new car?" Michael suggested. "Better to ask questions than to try and guess what the other person is thinking."

Ellie stifled a laugh. "That sounds like—"

"Yes," Michael stopped her, "Dating for Dummies, but it does seem applicable given the circumstances."

"It's actually a good idea," Olivia agreed, her thumbs flying across the virtual keyboard.

"You know, speaking of Whitney—" Ellie began.

A smile formed on Michael's face. "Your arch-nemesis," he interjected.

Ellie gave Michael a look and then continued. "We only have *Whitney's* word that she never saw Hugo again. But two people corroborated Simon's story that he left the museum alone and never saw Hugo again. What if Hugo did go back to the hotel, and Whitney is lying?"

"And what?" Michael asked, already knowing where this was heading.

"And she killed him," Ellie replied, annoyed that he would question something so obvious.

Michael shook his head in disagreement. "Whitney is tiny. You honestly think she could overpower Hugo?"

"Maybe she killed him in his sleep," Ellie proposed.

"And did what with his body? Put it in the hotel ice dispenser?" Michael leaned back and nearly fell off the picnic bench, forgetting he wasn't in a chair.

"Maybe it's still there," Olivia chimed in. "She hid his body in her room."

"Or," Ellie jumped in, "Whitney and Simon waited for him in the parking lot and hit him over the head with a tire iron and stuffed him in the trunk."

"Seriously...." Michael shook his head. "This is going from bad to worse."

"And that's why Simon got a new car," Olivia insisted.

"Because the dealership's not gonna notice a little thing like a body in the trunk?" Michael looked from Ellie to Olivia. "And you guys think I'm the crazy one."

"No, they dump the body before taking the car back. The dealership gets the car, unaware a crime has been committed, cleans it, and does whatever they do, and Bob's your uncle. You gotta think outside the box." Olivia grinned.

"I think I'm going to need that second drink," Michael moaned. "First, Uber is going to drop him off at the main entrance of the hotel, not in the middle of the parking lot. Also, that's a busy parking lot. You can't just hit someone over the head and manhandle them into the trunk of a tiny compact car."

"They could have waited for him upstairs in Whitney's room, and killed him there," Ellie suggested.

"Again, how do you move a body through a hotel, into a parking lot without being seen? It just doesn't make sense," said Michael as he massaged his temples.

"Easy, they're working for the museum," Olivia answered. "They could easily get a trunk or some type of shipping container, put him in that, and wheel it through the hotel on a luggage cart. Trade show people are always pushing those things through the lobby."

"Olivia, two words: Black Prius," Michael stated flatly. "A tiny little car, with a tiny trunk. There is no way you could transport a container large enough to hold a man the size of Hugo in that car."

"Plus," Michael added, "don't you find it a little suspicious that Whitney is throwing Simon under the bus? If they both attacked Hugo, why would she suddenly start pointing a finger at Simon?"

"That's easy," insisted Olivia, "to cast blame on him. Maybe there's some evidence in his old car that she knows about but can't say outright, something that connects Simon to the murder. Only she can't say anything, or she'd be admitting to knowledge of the crime."

"She's hoping we'll put the pieces together, or the police will," Ellie reasoned.

"I know you don't like our idea, Michael, but if their room is on the ground floor, they could have waited till the middle of the night and pushed the body out of the window, and then put it in the car."

"Just sounds too risky to me," Michael concluded. "Let me think about it before we jump to conclusions."

"We're just trying to talk things out, Michael," said Olivia, a tinge of annoyance in her voice.

"Did Whitney reply?" Ellie asked, attempting to change the dynamics of the conversation.

"Yes...well not much of a response. She pretty much reiterated that she thought the new rental car was suspicious. I'll thank her and tell her I'll pass the information on to my uncle."

Michael rested an arm on the warm wooden railing and gazed out at the ocean. "The exhibit is from seven to nine tonight," he said, thinking aloud. "Which means Simon and Whitney will be at the museum. It's six-fifteen now," he said, looking at his watch.

Ellie and Olivia leaned in, curious where Michael was going with his extrapolations.

"Look, I'm sorry. Something has obviously happened to Hugo. He's a textbook narcissist. His world evolves around self-adulation. There is no way he would miss opportunities to feed his ego."

"Dear Lord, Michael, quit bloviating and get to the point," Ellie exclaimed.

"Fine, if we really want to find out what happened, there are two things that need to be done. One may be a little illegal; the other will require my stunning wit and my charm."

Olivia sucked in sharply. "I think I'm going to be sick."

Chapter 20

Charming as an Olive

"You want to break into their hotel room?" Ellie put her face in her hands. "Michael West, you're going to give me an ulcer."

"It's the only way we can disprove your assumption that Hugo was attacked and is in one of their rooms."

"And your second idea?" Olivia asked hesitantly.

"We find out where Simon rented his car and see if there's anything amiss."

Olivia was just about to comment when a young man approached their table in black shorts and a black short-sleeved collared shirt. A thin line of perspiration stretched across his tanned forehead, just below his thick, cropped, white-blond hair.

"Evening, everyone, I'm Mark. I'll be your server. Is everyone okay on drinks?"

"We're great, thank you," Ellie piped in.

Olivia placed her phone on the table and took the last sip of her Mai Tai.

"Wonderful." Mark removed a pad from his pocket and clicked the pen on his chest. "I'll start with the ladies. Ma'am," he said, tilting his head toward Ellie, "what would you like?"

"I'd like the grilled sea bass, with corn on the cob and green beans, please, and an iced tea, unsweetened."

"And you, miss?" He turned his attention to Olivia.

"I'll take the fried flounder, onion rings, a side of fries, and a small salad with low-fat balsamic vinaigrette."

"Certainly. Anything to drink?" He looked up from his pad.

"Yes, an iced tea as well, with a wedge of lemon, unsweetened."

"And for the gentleman?"

"I'll have the grilled mahi-mahi. I'm on a diet, so can I just have one mahi?"

"Clever," Mark laughed, pleasing Michael. "And for your sides?"

"A Caesar salad. Oh, yes, I would also like a dirty martini, please."

"Excellent choice, sir," Mark nodded.

"I'm curious, Mark...I know this may come as a surprise, seeing I'm obviously debonair and sophisticated, but I don't drink martinis too often."

"He's more an appletini kind of guy," snorted Olivia.

Michael rolled his eyes in mock disgust. "I apologize, Mark, but what is it that makes a martini dirty?"

Mark searched Michael's face to see if there was a punch line to a joke coming, but Michael stared back with an inquisitive expression.

"Very well, the olives are what give the martini its crisp, complex taste. Without them, you would simply be drinking vodka, with a splash of vermouth."

"I see. Thank you so much, Mark, very educational." Michael smiled appreciatively.

"Certainly, sir. Let me know if there's anything else you need."

Michael turned to Olivia and Ellie, obviously pleased with himself. "So," he said, clasping his hands as if closing a deal. "Olives, though small and unassuming, are what give the martini its complex, crisp taste."

"I always thought it was the alcohol," Olivia shrugged. "I usually just toss the olives."

Ellie nodded in agreement, stuffing a hushpuppy in her mouth. "Pretty sure it's the alcohol."

For the second time that night, Olivia's phone jumped to life. She quickly wiped her fingers on a napkin and answered the phone.

"She's quite popular," Michael whispered to Ellie. "We may need new agents."

"It's Louie," Olivia whispered out the side of her mouth.

"I wonder if he found something," Ellie whispered.

Ellie and Michael sat staring at each other in silence. Michael could hear snippets of Louie's dry, gravelly voice.

"You guys aren't going to believe this," Olivia exclaimed as she ended the call. "Hugo never scheduled an Uber."

Ellie thought for a moment. "Maybe Simon just assumed Hugo was using Uber. He could have used Lyft or the local taxi service. Would be an easy mistake."

Olivia was already shaking her head. "Louie said there were no ride services dispatched to the museum after ten last night, except for ours."

"So, where did he go?" Ellie mused.

"No one knows. Louie and Detective Mitchell are on the way to the museum right now to speak to Simon and Whitney. He said he'd ask him about the car."

"Good luck," Michael stated. "The exhibit starts in fifteen minutes—they're going to be swamped."

Mark arrived at their table, his arms lined with plates. He served Ellie and then Olivia. "I'll be right back with the rest of the food and your drinks."

"Thank you, Mark," Olivia sighed, breathing in the aroma of her fried flounder.

Moments later, he returned with the rest of the food and Michael's dirty martini, served in a plastic cup. Three olives, impaled by a plastic sword, rested against the inside.

"Fancy." Olivia chortled, eyeing Michael's drink.

"This is delicious," Ellie declared, enjoying a bite of her grilled sea bass. "Just the right amount of seasoning—it practically melts in your mouth."

"Looks delicious." Olivia nodded. "The flounder is really good, too. How's your mahi, Michael?"

"Cooked to perfection. I have to admit, they do an amazing job here." He took a sip of his martini and made a face. "That's strong."

"Admit it," she laughed, "you would have preferred the appletini."

His face broke into an embarrassed smile. "You know me all too well. Olivia, may I see that picture of Simon's rental car again?"

"Sure." She jabbed her password into the phone and slid it across the table to Michael. "What are you thinking?"

"There're two places to rent a car around here—the airport and Curtis Automotive." He zoomed in on the photo, expanding the image with his forefinger and thumb. "I'm actually surprised," Michael said, looking up from the phone. "He rented the car from Curtis Automotive; I would have thought they would have used the airport."

He turned the phone and showed them the plastic license plate covering with the words Curtis Automotive on the top and their phone number on the bottom.

"Do you mind if I Google Curtis Automotive?" Michael asked, before clicking the browser icon.

"Not at all," Olivia replied.

"Darn." He shook his head after searching on Google. "Rental service and garage close at seven."

"Yeah." Ellie nodded. "Their convenience store and gas pumps are open till midnight."

"Actually, the fact that the rental department closes at seven might be a good thing. If Simon returned to the hotel about an hour ago, chances are they haven't had a chance to service his car. If he left any clues—"

"They might still be there," Olivia offered, finishing his sentence.

Michael pulled out his wallet and motioned Mark over.

"Let me get it tonight," Ellie said. "You've helped us out in the café the past two days. Our treat."

Michael hesitated, and then put his card back in his wallet. "Okay. Thank you so much, Ellie."

"Certainly, Michael. *Olive you*." She winked.

Chapter 21

Dollars For Your Thoughts?

It was 7:45 when Ellie eased her car into the Curtis Automotive parking lot. Michael had fired off a flurry of texts from the back seat and then insisted that they make a quick detour to the Steele Investigation Group's office. He alluded to a couple of items that he had to pick up before continuing.

The Curtis Automotive complex consisted of a tasteful sandstone-colored building with green trim and giant windows stretched out in front of them. Three large bay doors, with small rectangular windows, connected to the main building, and behind the doors was a state-of-the-art garage.

Ellie backed into a parking space at the end of a long row of cars, designated for rental vehicles. A single light shone behind one of the garage doors.

Olivia's phone dinged. "Simon said the check engine light was coming on in his car—that's why he turned it in. Louie said he'll send someone over first thing in the morning to check out his story."

Michael pointed out that there was a light on in the garage. "Someone's still working; tomorrow morning may be too late. I'm going to check the rental cars to see if I see Simon's," he said, climbing out of the back seat. "I'll be right back."

Michael closed the car door and surveyed the gas pumps. There were a couple of patrons pumping gas, but no one was paying attention to him. He casually walked between the rows of rentals. He spotted a white Prius and a metallic-blue Prius, but not a black one. Maybe he had rented his previous car from the airport and got the new one from here. It didn't really make sense, but he didn't see Simon's car anywhere.

He turned to Ellie and Olivia and held up one finger, signaling for them to give him a minute, and then he gestured toward the garage. He scanned the lot once again, and then walked to the third bay door that was lit from inside. He stood on his toes and peeked into one of the windows. A man in green overalls and a baseball cap was operating a piece of machinery connected to a black Prius. Michael pulled his phone from his pocket and called Ellie.

"Ellie," he spoke softly. "I see Simon's car. The mechanic's got a computer hooked to it."

"What are you going to do?"

"I'm going to rely on my wit and charm to see if he'll talk to me."

"Yeah, about that, maybe you should let your wallet do the talking."

Michael rolled his eyes and ended the call. He rapped on the door with his knuckles. The mechanic looked up and then waved him away, mouthing the words *we're closed*. He turned back to his computer, jabbing greasy fingers at his keyboard.

Michael pulled his wallet from his back pocket, reached inside, and removed a couple of twenties. He stretched them across the window so the mechanic could see. The mechanic eyed the money, shook his head, and angrily shooed him away.

Great, now what? He searched his wallet; he had a ten and two fives—not exactly compelling. Michael paced in front of the door, thinking. "ATM," he said aloud, noticing the green neon letters glowing in the front window, beckoning him into the convenient store. He scurried off and returned a few minutes later with a handful of twenties.

He carefully fanned out one hundred dollars and spread them across the window. This time when he knocked, the man left his perch, sauntered over, and unlocked the door.

"Thank you." Michael lowered his eyes to the man's name, embroidered on his overalls pocket. "Raymond. That's a name I haven't heard in a while."

Raymond sighed, his eyebrows raised, high above his almond-colored eyes. "What can I help you with, mister? I'm kind of in the middle of something." His voice was soft, with a strong southern drawl. His eyes stared hungrily at the money in Michael's hand.

"A gentleman named Simon Parker brought this car in today." He pointed to the black Prius. "He works for me at the Lana Cove Museum," Michael lied. "I hate to do this to him, but Simon's been acting really strange lately. There've been some thefts at the museum, and this morning he called and said that his check engine light was coming on, and he wouldn't make it in for work."

"And you want to know if he's lying," Raymond concluded smugly.

"Yes."

Raymond held out an oil-stained hand. "My old lady's anniversary is next week," he said, taking the bills from Michael. He slowly folded the money and placed it in his pocket.

"Well, I hope that helps." Michael gestured to Raymond's pocket.

"The answer is yes," Raymond said flatly.

"Yes, it will help, or yes, he's lying?"

"Both. Now, I've answered your question." He motioned for Michael to leave. "I've gotta finish up here so I can—"

"Wait, Raymond, do you mind if I check out the car?"

Raymond worked his mouth a moment as if chewing on what to say.

"I need to make sure there's nothing from the museum in there. If you don't mind," Michael offered, hoping that a reason would make it easier for him to say yes.

A knowing smile played across Raymond's face. Once again he held out his hand.

At this rate, the missis is going to have a great anniversary. Michael reached in his pocket and peeled off another sixty dollars.

Raymond looked at the bills and shook his head.

"Okay, another forty," Michael said, trying to take control of the negotiation, "but I get to check out the car and the trunk."

"Fair enough," Raymond agreed.

Michael added another forty to the stack of bills, and Raymond pocketed them with a huge smile. He tilted his head to the car. "You got five minutes."

Michael hurried over to the car and climbed inside. He opened the middle console and the glove compartment. They were both empty except for the car's owner manual.

He pulled a UV flashlight from his pocket and shone it on the seat and the floorboard. Nothing. He turned and faced the back seat and waved the flashlight across the seat and the floor in the back, but it was clean.

Michael pulled himself out of the car, careful not to hit the door against the computer that was connected to the car by a series of red and black wires.

"Diagnostics system," Raymond said. "We check to make sure there are no mechanical issues with the car. Then we do a basic factory reset on the computer system."

"Does that include the car's GPS system?"

Raymond's beady eyes gleamed greedily. "Is this a work-related question?"

"Well, if I could see where Simon was instead of work, that, of course, would be very—"

Raymond held out his hand once more.

"Yeah, yeah," Michael replied. "I feel like I'm going to be buying your fiancé a new house."

"Information's expensive," Raymond smiled.

Reluctantly, Michael fished the remaining bills out of his pocket. "Before I hand over the money, you answer the questions first. He held the money aloft so Raymond could see the five bills.

"Okay, fair enough."

"Can you retrieve the GPS data?"

"Yes."

"Will you retrieve it for me?"

"No"

"Why not?" Michael asked, annoyed.

"I've already deleted it."

"Why did you delete it? Did Simon tell you to delete the information?"

"We reset the computer on all rental cars to protect our clients' information."

"What information? Besides GPS data, what could a rental car possibly—"

"Have you ever paired your cell phone with a rental car?"

"Yeah…why?"

"When you rent a car and pair your phone with it, the computer retains a lot of information from your phone."

"Like what?"

"GPS coordinates, your contact lists, the numbers for any calls that you made, text messages, sometimes even your garage access code."

"All of that information is stored in this car?" Michael asked excitedly.

"Was." Raymond smiled, knowing where Michael was headed. "I wiped it clean."

"Is there any way to get it back?"

"Sorry, mister, once it's gone, it's gone." He held out his hand. "I believe I've answered all of your questions. I'd really like to finish up here so I can leave."

"Just one second," Michael said, "and then I'll be out of your hair." He hurried over to the car, climbed inside, and pressed the trunk-open button on the key remote. He hopped out, flicked on his UV flashlight, and began inspecting the trunk. Nothing. He pulled up the carpet, removed the tire iron, and shone the light on it. There was no reaction; it was clean. Just as he was closing the trunk, he noticed a small piece of black plastic caught in the locking mechanism. He carefully teased the piece of plastic loose and folded it inside his ATM receipt.

"All right, Mr. Museum Man...your time's up."

"Thank you, Raymond." Michael nodded. "You've been a big help." His foot had barely cleared the doorway when Raymond forcefully shut the door behind him and locked it.

Chapter 22

A Piece of Evidence?

"We were too late," Michael said as he climbed into the back seat of Ellie's car. "Raymond, their ever-efficient mechanic, erased everything."

"What does that even mean?" Ellie asked as she pulled out of the Curtis Automotive parking lot.

"When a rental car is brought back in, it's washed, detailed, and vacuumed and a factory reset is done on the car's computer. So, any data like GPS or mobile phone information is erased to protect the renter."

"Oh…," Ellie replied. That one word said it all.

"What about the check engine light? Did the mechanic remember if that was on?" Olivia asked, her voice hopeful.

"He said that the engine was fine. That there were no alerts."

"So, Simon lied," Olivia concluded.

"It appears so." Michael nodded. "I did a thorough check of the car for evidence. I checked the glovebox, between and under the seats, and the center console."

"What about the tire iron? Did you check that?" Ellie asked.

"There was a tire repair kit in the trunk with a miniature jack and the world's smallest tire iron in a satchel. I don't think it had ever been opened."

"But you did check it?" Ellie asked.

"Of course. I even checked the entire vehicle with my UV penlight to check for blood, but I didn't find anything."

"UV penlight?" Olivia inquired.

Michael held up his keychain. "It's a lifesaver when you stay in hotel rooms. I really don't want to go into detail."

"Yeah," Olivia replied, "sorry I asked."

"Well, it's still very suspicious. Simon obviously lied about the check engine alert, and he seemed to be in a hurry to get rid of the car," Ellie surmised.

"I agree. Oh, and I found this." Michael passed the folded ATM slip to Olivia. She carefully unfolded the receipt.

"It looks like a piece of plastic from a heavy-duty trash bag."

"I think so too," Michael agreed. "It was caught up in the trunk's locking mechanism.

Ellie eased up to a stoplight. "Let me see."

Olivia passed the strip of plastic to Ellie. "Either that or a piece of tarp."

Michael's mind immediately went to a tarp: Simon and Whitney rolling Hugo up inside like a carpet. *But again, how would they get Hugo's body out of the hotel?* "I'm sorry," Michael apologized, "what were you saying?"

"I'm amazed the mechanic gave you all of that information and let you search the car," Olivia repeated.

"Oh, yeah, that." Michael crossed his arms across his chest. "Like I said, you guys underestimate my ability to get people to talk."

"That's got to be it," Olivia smiled. "I'm sure it had nothing to do with this," she said, smiling as she handed Michael his ATM receipt.

Chapter 23

The Break-in

Ellie eased off of A1A into the Bay Breeze Hotel parking lot. The oceanfront hotel was sandy brown, with sweeping balconies encircling the building. Every room was oceanfront. Royal blue spotlights swept across the face of the building, mimicking waves rolling across the shore. Calypso music filled the air. A private swath of beach lay just beyond the doors behind the hotel. A sign in the parking lot offered overflow parking behind the souvenir shop across the street.

"There's a space," Olivia pointed out.

Ellie nodded and maneuvered through the packed parking lot to a tiny space for compact cars, directly next to the sea barrier.

"This thing must be a nightmare to get in and out of," Olivia observed.

Michael checked his watch. It was eight-thirty. The exhibit ended at nine. They would have just enough time to get in and leave before Whitney and Simon left the museum.

Ellie disconnected her phone from the car charger and slipped it into her purse. Without a word, the trio exited the car and walked toward the hotel. She paused when they reached the main entrance. "Michael, are you sure this is going to work?" Ellie asked.

"We'll be in and out in no time," Michael replied confidently. "We just need to stick to the plan."

The plan was simple. Find an employee who could access hotel guest information and bribe them with cash. Michael had stopped by the local Ship and Save and grabbed two FedEx envelopes to add some authenticity to his cover story. A cover story he declined to reveal—that was not fully developed. While Ellie and Michael executed the plan, Olivia would wait in the hotel lobby and keep an eye out for Simon and Whitney.

"Wish us luck." Ellie smiled nervously as they headed for a row of elevators.

Due to a town ordinance, like all structures in Lana Cove, the hotel had a maximum limit of three floors. It wasn't until they reached the third floor that they found a young man delivering room service.

"This might be our chance," Michael whispered.

A young man with dark blond hair, dressed in black pants and a white collared shirt, held a circular tray in one hand and a slip of paper in his other hand. "Cheapskates," he hissed, staring at the receipt. The young man's mouth flew open in surprise when he realized he wasn't alone in the hallway. His face turned bright red in embarrassment.

"I'm so sorry, I shouldn't have said that. It's my third time to their room in the past twenty minutes, and then they didn't tip me," he explained.

Ellie gave him an understanding smile. She looked at his nametag. "It's okay, Patrick, it's our little secret. I'm in the restaurant business too, and I can't tell you how many times I've been stiffed."

"You would think that people on their vacation would be a little more considerate."

"Do you work here full-time?" Ellie asked.

"I'm part-time. I go to Lana Cove College during the day and work here at night."

"That's dedication." Michael smiled. "Wait a minute, maybe you could help us, and we could help you," Michael exclaimed as if he'd just come up with the idea on the spot. He held up the two FedEx envelopes. "We've got two VIP tickets for the new exhibit at the Lana Cove Museum. We were supposed to meet our friends here, to give them the tickets, but they're running late."

"Okay." Patrick cocked his head to the side. "How can I help?"

"Well, since those jerks stiffed you, how about one hundred dollars?" He reached into his pocket and counted off five twenties. "If you can help us find our friend's room, we'll just slide the tickets under their doors." Michael held up the FedEx envelopes again.

"Did you say one hundred dollars?" Patrick grinned, not able to believe his luck.

"Yep," Ellie replied. "We just need the room numbers for Whitney Cooper and Simon Parker. You can even come with us if you'd like."

"You're just sliding the envelopes under their door, right?" Patrick clarified.

"That's it." Michael looked at his watch. "I'll throw in an extra twenty if you hurry."

"You got it. Wait right here, I'll be right back."

True to his word, five minutes later, Patrick returned with a yellow sticky note. "Here's their room numbers." He handed Ellie the paper.

"Thank you so much," Michael exclaimed. "Did you want to accompany us?"

"Is it okay if I don't?" Patrick asked, concern spreading across his face. "I don't want to make my boss mad at me."

"Oh no." Ellie touched his shoulder. "Get back to work." She smiled kindly at him. "I hope you have a much better night."

Ellie and Michael took the elevator to the second floor and stepped into the hallway. The carpet was a deep ocean blue color, the walls sand-brown, with blue accent lighting along the ceiling.

"Two-sixteen is to our left," Ellie said, reading a golden placard located on the wall directly across from the elevators.

Michael glanced at his watch; it was ten minutes to nine. He picked up his pace, eyeing room numbers as they traveled deeper into the hallway.

"Are you sure this is going to work?" Ellie took in a deep breath, hurrying to keep up with Michael's long strides.

Michael removed what looked like an ordinary dry erase marker from his pants pocket. "According to Damon Steele, this gadget will open just about any hotel room door."

"That's a bit unsettling," Ellie replied.

"What's unsettling is any thirteen-year-old with a basic understanding of electronics could make this thing for less than thirty dollars."

"There it is, 216," Ellie said softly. She nervously glanced over her shoulder, checking the hallway behind them.

Michael quickly put on a pair of blue latex gloves and handed Ellie a pair. He removed the "Do Not Disturb" sign that hung over the handle of the lock and put it in his pocket. He knelt in front of the door and popped the top off the dry erase marker. Instead of a felt tip, there was a circular metal probe that extended about a half an inch. He inserted the probe into the base of the lock. There was a slight buzz, and then the familiar metallic click of a door being unlocked.

"Holy Moses," Ellie whispered, "it worked."

Michael was just as shocked as she was. He pushed the door open, and they slipped inside Simon's room. Ellie quickly pulled and locked it behind them.

The first thing that hit them was the smell of industrial-strength cleaner.

"That will take your breath away," Michael exclaimed, making a face.

Ellie nodded her agreement.

The bathroom was to their immediate right, a king-sized bed stood in the center of the room, and a pastel painting of a lighthouse hung just above the headboard. The TV remote lay atop a sea of blankets.

A dresser, television, and workstation were nestled against the wall opposite the bed. A deep blue fabric chair sat in the corner, facing the sliding glass doors, leading out to the balcony, revealing a view of the ocean.

"Okay, first, we establish that Hugo isn't here," he said.

Ellie nodded. She stepped into the bathroom, praying that she wouldn't find a body on ice. Michael heard the shower curtain open, and a sigh of relief.

He dropped to his knees, feeling a bit ridiculous that he was checking under the bed. The frame was a mere six inches from the floor; there was no way they could hide a body there.

Ellie crossed the room and opened a closet. It was filled with shirts, a suit jacket, and a safe mounted to the floor.

"Okay," Michael said, dusting off his hands. "We've established that Hugo is not in this room. Check the rest of the room, see if you see anything suspicious. I'm going to get us into the safe." Michael looked at his watch; it was five to nine.

Ellie didn't bother asking. She moved around the room, checking drawers and sifting through his suitcase.

Michael picked up the phone handset and pressed zero. A moment later a woman's voice answered the line. "Good evening, Mr. Parker, how may I help you?"

"Good evening. Our safe isn't working and we have a dinner reservation for nine. Is there any way that someone could help us? Better sooner than later," he added.

"Certainly, I'll send maintenance right up."

"Wonderful. I'll make sure to put in a good word with your GM for you," he added and hung up.

"Michael," Ellie exclaimed, "are you crazy?"

"Not at all. Hotel safes are notoriously kludgy. No one's going to suspect anything." He handed the television remote to Ellie. "Find a show and pretend like you're getting ready to go out. I'll handle the maintenance guy."

A squawk from a walkie-talkie alerted Michael and Ellie of the man's arrival before he had a chance to knock. Michael waited a beat and then opened the door. A bestubbled, middle-aged man wearing a black t-shirt and khaki pants stood in the hallway. His lips bent in an upside-down *U*, conveying a permanent look of annoyance.

"I'm so sorry to be a bother." Michael stepped aside, inviting the man into the room. "I keep getting an error code on the safe." He reached into his pocket and pulled out a twenty. "Here, this is for your trouble."

The man murmured a thanks and eagerly snatched the twenty from Michael. Ellie maneuvered behind Michael. "See, honey? He'll have it opened in no time. I'm sure he does this a dozen times a night."

"At least," said the man as he knelt in front of the safe.

"Just so you know, if you hold down the lock button for eight seconds and then type in six zeros, it will unlock. So, if this happens again, you don't need to call me. Unless you like handing out twenties."

"Good to know." Michael smiled.

"A lot of hotels never bother to reset the default keycode sequence, including this one," continued the man as he backed out of the closet. "It's all set. Have a good night."

"You too." Michael waved. He shut the door behind the maintenance man and set the bolt lock.

Ellie darted into the closet and crouched in front of the safe.

"Anything?" Michael asked excitedly.

"A passport and a cell phone." Ellie held up the two items.

Michael took a look at the phone, and his mind instantly flashed back to the night at the museum: Hugo smacked Simon's hand, the phone slid across the floor. Michael had picked it up, letting Simon know he had it...only this wasn't the same phone.

"Simon has two phones," Michael said excitedly.

"Why do you think he would need two phones?"

"Secrets," Michael declared. He pressed the side of the phone; a micro card popped out. Michael dashed across the room, opened the lid on Simon's laptop, and swiped his finger across the mouse pad. "Password protected."

"Not surprised," Ellie said.

Michael snatched his iPhone from his pocket. *Dang, no SD slot.*

Ellie shook her head, already knowing the question. "Livs and I both have iPhones."

"Of course," Michael said, pacing around the room. "Ellie, I'm going to make a quick phone call. Put the phone and passport back inside the safe, but don't lock it."

Ellie nodded and disappeared into the closet. Michael slid his finger across his phone, opened his contacts, and called Damon Steele. Two minutes later, they were in the hotel lobby. Ellie motioned for Olivia to follow them outside.

"What's going on?" Olivia asked, her eyes wide with curiosity. "It's five after nine—shouldn't we be going?"

"Ellie can fill you in. I'll be right back." Michael hurried off through the parking lot, disappearing across A1A.

Chapter 24

Run!

"Damon Steele was able to copy everything over," Michael said, holding a tiny memory card in his hand.

"Awesome," Ellie replied. "We've—"

A car swung into the parking lot, momentarily blinding them with its headlights. Michael ushered them against the wall, into the shadow of the hotel.

"It's okay," Olivia breathed, "it's not either of their cars."

"All right, I'm going to run upstairs and return his SD card. If either Simon or Whitney return, do whatever you've got to do to delay them."

"Just hurry," Ellie insisted. "I'd like to be gone before they return!"

Michael spun on his heel and hurried through the lobby. It felt like an eternity, but finally, an elevator opened. He stepped inside, jabbed the number two button, and then pressed the door closed button. Repeatedly. *This thing is so slow I should've taken the stairs.* He glanced up at the ceiling; his reflection stared back at him. Hugo said he liked to live his adventures and not write about them...if only he could see Michael now.

The elevator jolted slightly, coming to a stop at the second floor. Michael dashed from the elevator and hurried down the hall. A couple of tourists, pulling their luggage behind them, moved at a snail's pace ahead of him. Luckily, they were talking loudly and looking for their room. They were oblivious that Michael was just a few paces behind them.

Michael arrived at 216, checked the hallway, and knelt in front of the lock. Seconds later, he was in Simon's room. He slipped the SD card back into Simon's phone, then pulled out his own phone and took pictures of Simon's passport.

He glanced at his watch. "Nine twenty," he said aloud.

Michael stood in the doorway of the closet. *If I shut the safe, then Simon won't be able to get in because his code will no longer work.* Michael's brain whirred at high speed. *If he can't get in, then he'll call the front desk, and they'll be wondering why his safe isn't working again—and what if they sent the same maintenance worker, and there's a different man in the room.* Michael tapped his hand nervously on his leg. *What should I do?*

In the end, he decided to shut the safe but not completely close it. Perhaps Simon would think that he didn't close it all the way when he left. Otherwise, through a conversation with the maintenance worker, he would easily be able to figure out who had been in his room. Michael closed the door to the closet and slipped out of Simon's room into the hallway.

He hurried down the hallway to room 219; he'd only be a second. Michael inserted the unlocking device and then slipped into Whitney's room. The rich vanilla smell of Whitney's perfume still hung in the air. He didn't need to pull back the shower curtain—it was already open. A damp towel hung over the curtain rod. Two toothbrushes lay on a washcloth, and next to it lay an electric razor. Hugo had indeed been staying with her.

He quickly moved to the bedroom. The only place you could hide a body was the closet, and he wasn't surprised to find the only occupants were her clothes and Hugo's clothes. Michael's eyes swept over the room. A desk, a trashcan beneath, a vase filled with purple and pink flowers, a laptop, and a notebook. *I'll come back to the notebook,* he thought.

Michael opened the blue and white curtains, revealing a set of sliding glass doors and the balcony. He quickly slid the doors open and stepped outside. The calypso music from the pool floated up to him.

Just beyond the pool, in the semi-darkness, he could make out the beach and the ocean.

Something pulled at the back of his mind. *What was it?* Just as he stepped back inside and pulled the curtain closed, his phone buzzed. It was a text from Olivia. *The police are here get out.*

Police? Michael panicked. *Why would the police be here? Had someone seen him?* Michael pressed the microphone button. *Meet me across the street. I'm taking the stairs.* He pressed "Send," then dashed across the room. The squawk of a walkie-talkie just outside the door brought him to a stop.

"I'm opening it now," said a gruff male voice.

Michael spun around in a circle, trying to figure out what to do. *Should I try jumping from the balcony to the pool? How far is it down—thirty feet?* He grabbed a baseball hat that read Egyptian Airlines and pulled it on, covering his eyes. There was an electronic chirp, and then the door began to open.

Michael did the only thing he could do. He yanked the door open, catching the security guard by surprise, and smacked him in the face with a massive pillow. The man staggered backward into the wall. Behind him, he heard the ding of the elevator.

"Stop!" the security guard screamed.

Michael raced down the hallway, crashing into the door that led to the stairs. He slammed his knee and hip painfully into the railing but didn't stop. The door above swung open. He could hear the *smack smack* of the security guard's leather soles on the stairs.

Michael reached the last step, leaped across the landing, and threw his shoulder into the door. He burst outside, twisting his head left to right—*dumpsters, parking lot, police cruiser*. He sprinted to the parking lot and ducked behind a red Mustang, just as the security guard burst through the door, screaming into his walkie-talkie.

Michael didn't wait to see what happened next. He hurried through the rows of cars, crouching as he ran. The lot ended at a large concrete wall that surrounded a condo project. Michael climbed onto the hood of a car, triggering the car alarm.

"Great," Michael muttered. He leaped through the air, his hands just reaching the top of the wall. Gripping the top, he swung his legs back and forth like a pendulum, the rough concrete biting deep into the palm of his hands.

"Come on!" he yelled to himself. He swung once again, throwing his right leg up and out. His foot made it to the top of the wall. Using his leg and what little strength he had left in his arms, he pulled himself up and over, sending him crashing to the ground on the other side. He lay in the grass for a moment, motionless, trying to catch his breath.

From the other side of the wall, he could hear the scrambling of footsteps. He pushed himself up and scoured the condo parking lot. It wouldn't take the police long to figure out where he'd gone. Another squad car raced by, blue lights flashing.

Michael's phone buzzed in his pocket. He crouched behind a car to read Ellie's text. *Are you okay?*

Yes, he replied. *Be there in a minute.*

Michael jogged around the massive condo complex, through the parking lot, and then dashed across A1A. Slipping behind a string of stores, he made his way to Ellie's car, parked in the shadows of Ned's Souvenir Shop.

"What the heck?" Olivia exclaimed angrily when Michael got in the car. "Are you trying to get arrested?"

Michael leaned forward in his seat, his face in his hands as a wave of nausea washed over him.

"Are you going to answer?" Olivia twisted angrily in her seat. Her expression changed, however, when she saw the blood dripping from Michael's hands onto his pants leg.

"Are you okay?" Olivia asked, her voice filled with worry.

"Yes," Michael nodded. His entire body ached. "I sort of ran into a railing, and then became intimate with a cement wall. We've got a date next Saturday."

"Yep, he's okay." Ellie sighed.

Olivia retrieved a handful of tissues from the glove compartment and handed them to Michael. "What happened up there?"

"Could we maybe talk and drive?" Michael peered anxiously out the window as another police cruiser whipped into the Bay Breeze parking lot.

"Good idea," Ellie replied. She started the car, swung around the parking lot, and pulled onto A1A. An unmarked police car flew past, blue lights flashing in its grill.

"Congratulations, Michael, you've managed to tie up the entire Lana Cove police force," Ellie said.

"Just think of me as job security," Michael said wryly.

"I think that was my uncle that just passed us." Olivia's phone rang, substantiating her comment. "I hate it when I'm right." She sighed. "What do I say?"

"Martini's," Michael said quickly, twisting in his seat, eyeing the bar's brightly glowing sign behind them. "We just had a drink at Martini's."

"Hi, Louie," Olivia's voice rang out. "I was just about to call you. We were at Martini's and heading home and we saw all of the commotion at the Bay Breeze. What's going on?"

Michael watched anxiously from the back seat as the Lana Cove Crime Scene Investigation vehicle passed by.

Michael, Ellie thought, *what did you do?*

Olivia pressed the speaker button on her phone so everyone could hear her conversation with Detective Adams.

"Detective Mitchell and I were just heading over to meet CSU to process Whitney Cooper's room when a call came in that a security guard had been attacked by a man inside her room."

"Oh no—is he okay?"

"Yes. He said the man pushed past him against the wall and fled."

"So, he got away?"

"For now. Don't worry, we'll find him."

Michael took in a deep breath. Detective Adams seemed so certain he'd catch his man.

"Listen, Whitney hasn't tried to contact you, has she?"

"No, not since she sent the picture of Simon's car."

"If she does, let me know right away. I've got to—
"

"Louie, why is CSU processing her room?"

"We received an anonymous tip that a man matching Hugo's description was seen on the balcony of Whitney's room this afternoon." Other voices crackled in the background.

"Look, Livs, I gotta go. I'll let you know what I find out. Stay safe and let me know if you hear anything from Whitney."

"I will." Olivia hung up the phone. She had so many questions to ask, but they would have to wait.

"An anonymous tip—what do you think that's all about?" Ellie asked.

"I don't know, maybe Whitney's lying, or maybe Hugo is hiding out somewhere at the hotel," Olivia suggested.

"That doesn't make any sense. Why? He has absolutely zero motive to suddenly disappear," Michael insisted.

"Right now, I think we need to figure out why Simon has a second phone, and what's on that SIM card," Olivia said.

"Agreed. My house?" Michael offered.

Ellie nodded. "Your house is the closest. You can tell us what you found out on the way."

Chapter 25

Michael's Hunch

Michael leaned catty-corner on the back seat of Ellie's car and stretched his aching legs out.

"Okay," Michael started, "I did everything just like we planned. I returned Simon's card and made sure his room was just like we'd found it."

He guessed by Ellie and Olivia's silence that he should continue.

"I checked my watch, figured I had a few more minutes before Whitney or Simon would arrive, so I decided to quickly check Whitney's room."

"Meanwhile the boys in blue arrived," Ellie added.

"Yes. I didn't panic, because I figured it was for something else. I did a quick check to make sure Hugo wasn't in the room, and just as I was about to leave, the security guard shows up at the door. And, by the way," Michael interrupted himself, "Whitney wasn't lying about Hugo staying there. His belongings were everywhere."

"Could you tell if he'd been there recently?"

"Sorry, Livs, didn't get a chance. I mean, I saw his toothbrush, clothes, and a suitcase, but nothing that really stood out."

"Michael," Ellie asked apprehensively, "did the guard see your face?"

"Ellie, you're not dealing with a novice. I snatched Hugo's baseball cap, swung the door open, and hit him with a pillow. He was completely caught off guard."

"You attacked him?" Olivia moaned and facepalmed her forehead.

"Attacked?" Michael asked incredulously. "I don't think attack is the right word choice. I hit him with a big fluffy white pillow. If it makes you feel better, I'll anonymously send him a fruit basket and a get-well card, okay?"

"So," Ellie confirmed, "he wouldn't be able to recognize you?"

"Impossible," Michael reassured Ellie. "I had this lovely baseball cap pulled down to the tip of my nose. The only thing he saw was a pillow, and then my shapely backside."

"Shapely," Ellie chuckled, feeling a surge of relief.

"Did you find anything in her room? Any clues?" Olivia asked.

"Not so much in her room, but I did find something out *about* her room."

"Enlighten us," Olivia said sarcastically.

"I'll explain, but it's more of a visual thing. Livs, can you send me the pics of Simon's new car?"

"Sure." Olivia navigated to the texts and forwarded the images to Michael. Seconds later, his phone buzzed.

"Perfect. Bear with me just a second, and if my hunch is right, I'll explain." Michael flicked back and forth between the two images. "Where were these pictures taken?"

"From Whitney's hotel room. Remember, she said Simon had just pulled into the hotel in a new rental car. So, I'm guessing from her hotel room or her balcony," Olivia deduced.

"Neither," Michael replied flatly. "Her balcony overlooks the pool, and you can't even see the parking lot from her room. And, there are no other windows in her room."

"All right, Sherlock, obviously you know something we don't. I'm simply going by what she told us," Olivia frowned.

"My gut also tells me that Whitney didn't take these pictures."

"Does this gut of yours have a hypothesis?" Olivia inquired.

"There are windows at the end of the hallway," Ellie interjected. "Maybe she saw him pull up and took the picture from there."

"Not unless she has a Nikon D90," Michael smiled. Olivia turned toward the back seat, a baffled look on her face.

"Look, either you begin explaining yourself without the dramatic pauses, or I'm going to bludgeon you with something much harder than a pillow."

"Fine," Michael capitulated. "Remember when we came to the conclusion that Whitney might be working with someone?"

"Yes," Olivia and Ellie replied in unison.

"It was rhetorical. You didn't need to answer that."

"Michael West, I'm going to snap your dainty little writer fingers like twigs—"

"Sorry." Michael held up his hands in mock surrender. "I uploaded the two pictures to a photo website that displays the EXIF metadata stored in an image. EXIF data can tell you the date the photo was taken, the location, the type of camera used...you get the picture. No pun intended." Michael flipped his phone around so Olivia and Ellie could see the screen.

"That's frightening," Olivia said.

Ellie brought her car to a stop in front of Michael's house. A row of golden, solar-powered lanterns lit the driveway. Earl and Tammy, Michael's meddlesome neighbors, were sitting on their newly installed porch swing enjoying the evening. Ellie cut the engine so she wasn't blinding them with her headlights.

Michael leaned forward and rotated the knob that controlled her headlights, turning her brights on and blinding his neighbors.

"Michael," Ellie hissed, smacking his hand away. "Behave!"

Begrudgingly, Michael collapsed back into the car seat. "So," he continued dramatically, "who else do we know with a fancy camera and a chip on their shoulder?"

"Ivan Ware," Ellie and Olivia replied in unison.

"Exactly," Michael exclaimed. "Ivan Ware."

Chapter 26

Beautiful But Deadly

"Howdy, neighbor," Earl called out from his porch swing.

Michael continued walking toward the house as if he didn't hear them. "Scumbag," he whispered under his breath. Every time he saw Earl and Tammy, he was reminded of how they tried to steal his house from under him in a shady real estate deal. They were both in cahoots with the slimiest of slimeballs, real estate mogul Maxwell King.

"Why don't you build a massive fence, so you don't have to see them?" Ellie suggested.

"Or a moat," offered Olivia.

"Believe me," Michael assured Ellie, "I've thought about it." He unlocked the front door and flicked the lights on.

Olivia stifled a yawn. "I'm going to grab a glass of water if you don't mind."

"Help yourself," Michael called out. He cleared a stack of books and magazines from his sofa and invited Ellie to sit next to him. The ice maker rumbled in the kitchen.

Michael was about to warn Olivia that it was a bit overly enthusiastic when he heard an avalanche of ice crashing to the kitchen floor.

"I see you fixed the ice maker," Olivia called out from the kitchen.

"I may need to adjust the settings—it's a bit temperamental," he hollered back.

"Just a bit. I may need a Saint Bernard to guide me back to safety."

Michael imagined the large dog, the miniature barrel of scotch around its neck, pulling Olivia through the kitchen and into the living room.

"Michael." Ellie shook his arm. "The laptop."

"Yes, of course." He slid his laptop closer, flipped open the cover, and typed in his password. He inserted the SD card and waited for it to load.

Olivia joined them on the sofa, a mountain of ice spilling over the rim of her glass.

A window on Michael's laptop opened, displaying a series of drives. He double-clicked the memory card folder. It opened and revealed multiple directories, each identified by name. *Images, GPS, Texts, Contacts.*

Ellie and Olivia scooted in closer. Finally, they would see what Simon was up to.

Michael started by opening the images folder. There were three photos. He clicked on the first photo and expanded it.

"These two photos, are like the Egyptian seals on Baal's sarcophagus," Ellie said excitedly, pointing to the screen.

"I think they *are* the seals from the sarcophagus," Michael said as he pulled out his phone. He opened his phone's photo application and swiped through his images. "Found them. Ellie, check this number against the seals in the picture. One, three, three, seven, four, six, eight, one, B."

"It's a match," she confirmed.

"Open the other picture," Olivia said impatiently.

Michael opened the last image and zoomed in. "It's an x-ray."

"It's got to be an x-ray of Baal." Olivia pointed at the screen. "Those are his legs and there are...," she paused for a moment, "...two rectangular boxes on either side of him."

"Smuggling," Michael declared. "They must be smuggling...something...in Baal's sarcophagus."

"I think that we just found out why Simon was trying to keep from doing the CT scan," Olivia said.

"Hugo probably didn't know—" Ellie suggested.

"And he became suspicious when Simon wouldn't show him the pictures," Olivia finished Ellie's thought.

"Why would Simon take pictures of the seal and the x-ray?" Ellie asked.

"If he's smuggling goods...maybe as confirmation to the buyer?" Olivia proposed.

"Can we find out when these pictures were taken?"

"Just a second." Michael right-clicked an image of the Egyptian seal and selected properties from the pop-up screen. He scrolled down to creation date. The photo was taken nine days ago. For the latitude and longitude, he copied the coordinates and pasted them into the browser. "Luxor International Airport, in Egypt," Michael declared.

"What about the x-ray? When was that taken?" Ellie asked.

"Creation date is the same, time-stamped two hours after the seals photo," Michael said as he stared at his screen, confirming that the objects were in the sarcophagus after it was officially sealed.

Olivia's phone rang, startling everyone. "Hi, Louie. Everything okay? We're fine—dropping Michael off. I'm putting you on speaker so Ellie and Michael can hear."

"Sure. I'm on the way back to HQ. We've arrested Whitney."

"Arrested her?!" Olivia sat back, shocked. "Why?"

"We have reason to believe that she poisoned Hugo. We'll know more once we get the results back from forensics, but CSU found trace amounts of ground monkshood in a cup in her trashcan."

"Monkshood? I don't understand."

Michael began tapping away on his laptop as Detective Adams spoke. "It's a type of flower. Its roots are extremely poisonous. You do know what Whitney's background is, right? She's a specialist in herbology."

"Oh my God," Michael whispered, looking up from his laptop. "Those are the purple flowers I saw in Whitney's hotel room."

"What was that?" Detective Adams asked.

Olivia looked at Michael like she was about to murder him. "Nothing. Michael was just Googling Monkshood. He said it's a common flower found all over the US."

"Hi, Louie. So, you found the flowers and the cup in her room? Couldn't someone have planted them there?" Ellie asked.

"Hi, Ellie. Of course, that's always an option. However, we found an email on her phone where she purchased the flowers from a local florist, and both her fingerprints and Hugo's fingerprints are on the cup."

"Oh," Ellie whispered.

"We're bringing her in for questioning. I'll let you know what we find out."

"Wait, real fast," Olivia chimed in. "So, that puts Hugo at the hotel, right?"

"Yes. We're reviewing hotel video to establish a timeline."

"What about the museum video? How did he get to the hotel?" Michael asked.

"That's another story. We received the video files. They were nothing but hours of static, and the security guard didn't show up for work this morning. We're sending a unit over first thing in the morning to follow up. Listen, guys, I gotta run."

"Okay, please let us know what you find out. Have a good night," Olivia said.

"You too. I'm afraid it's gonna be a long one."

Chapter 27

The Game

The trio sat in silence after the phone call. They'd all been suspicious of Whitney, but now it just seemed too easy.

Michael was the first to break the silence. "So, if Hugo was poisoned at the hotel, what happened to his body? Who helped her?"

"Maybe her picture of the car was a cry for help?" Ellie offered.

"Yes, but we know that Ivan took the picture," Michael said. "He and Whitney had to be working together."

"My uncle's got people out looking for him right now. He obviously hasn't left Lana Cove because of the recent photo."

"I still don't understand why Whitney would kill him. She loses her lover, her job, and risks life in prison. Simon…well, he doesn't really lose anything. It's no secret that he had feelings for Whitney," Ellie declared.

"What?" Michael looked at Ellie, surprised by this revelation.

"Women's intuition. We have a feel for these things," she explained.

"And now," added Olivia, "he's running the show, and has a little smuggling operation going on."

"What about Ivan? Hugo crushed his career, embarrassed him in front of his peers." Ellie paused, thinking, *Is it enough to make someone become an accessory to murder?*

"To a lot of people, their career is their life, it's who they are. I know that people have certainly killed for less," Olivia said.

"So, you think she put us onto Simon to distract us from her?" Michael asked. "Maybe she knew about Simon's smuggling business and figured that we'd of course assume it was him."

"Right now, we're speculating." Ellie nodded to the laptop. "Let's find out what's in the other folders."

Michael clicked the GPS folder. "It's empty," he said, disappointed. "Damon said it would suck up all the data stored on the card."

"You've got me," Ellie shrugged. "It's my first SD card heist. Check the contacts folder."

Michael opened the contacts folder and clicked on the lone inhabitant. The document contained a single line of data: *Sender Unknown* and then ten digits. "Well, that was uneventful. I'm beginning to think this phone felt extremely undervalued."

"That's a Virginia area code," Ellie said. "I know it's a long shot—"

She didn't need to finish her thought. Michael copied the telephone number and pasted it into his browser. "It's a Cellular number, unlisted and connected to the Ultra Mobile Network, in Fairfax, Virginia."

"So, his one contact is most likely using a burner phone as well. I've never heard of Ultra Mobile Network," Olivia said.

"Probably a prepaid network," Michael guessed. He navigated back to the last folder and opened a file simply named *Texts*. There were three messages:

Departing, items secured, see attachments. D10121.jpg, D10122.jpg, D10123.jpg.

"You think those are—"

"Yep," said Michael, "look." He moved his cursor to the folder with the three photos. Their file names matched the file names in the text.

"So, he sent the text confirming that whatever he was shipping was safe. The timestamp is the same date as the photos," Ellie surmised.

Package arrived safely.

"The last text was from the other phone. *Drop point tomorrow, seven a.m.* That text is timestamped today!" Michael exclaimed.

"We've got to let my uncle know," Olivia insisted.

"Wait," Michael said, "his first question is going to be how we got this information."

Olivia's shoulders slumped. "What do we do?"

"We play the game," Michael grinned. "We make an anonymous call to your uncle and give him the information."

"How are we going...oh!" Olivia smiled. "A burner phone!"

"Let's go."

Thirty minutes later, Michael had installed a voice-changing application and called and left a message for Detective Adams. He followed up by calling dispatch and informing them that he had left an extremely important message for the detective regarding the Hugo Sebastian case. He finished the call and threw the phone in the dumpster in the Walgreens parking lot.

The trap was set.

Chapter 28

I've Got My Eyes On You

Ellie, Michael, and Olivia met Detective Adams at the Bitter Sweet Café at 5 a.m. Detective Adams looked haggard and annoyed. Except for a two-hour catnap, he'd been up all night. He informed them that he had received an anonymous tip that Simon was meeting with someone for a drop.

"What kind of drop?" Michael asked innocently.

"Don't know. We have a tracker on Simon's car, a man in the lobby, and another man across the street. Tech is running a live ping on his phones. There's no way he can slip through the cracks."

"Phones?" Ellie inquired nonchalantly, pretending like she knew nothing of the details of the anonymous call.

"Simon has two, one of them must be a burner phone." Detective Adams glanced at his phone. "Excuse me, I've gotta take this."

When Detective Adams returned to the table, his face was drawn tight. He took a sip of his coffee.

"Peyton Leek, the security guard from the museum, is dead."

"Dead?" Olivia gasped. "How?"

"Not sure. No sign of forced entry into his home. We were on our way to pick him up for questioning. Ran financials on him and found a five thousand dollar cash deposit."

Michael exhaled. "Sounds like his hush money. Shut him up permanently—no pun intended."

"I know the kid's father," Detective Adams said. "A little rough around the edges—got into trouble here and there."

"Know?" Ellie asked.

"He's still alive. He's in the Palmbrooks senior home. He was diagnosed with Alzheimer's about five years ago. He must have left Peyton the house." Detective Adams shook his head. "Life is never simple."

"Anything new from Whitney?" Michael inquired.

"Nothing, just insistence of innocence, that she loved Hugo and would never hurt him. Unfortunately, the evidence is building."

Detective Adams looked at his phone. "Simon's on the move. He's in the hotel lobby, with his luggage. Looks like he's checking out of the hotel. Won't be long now." He pushed back from the table and stood up. "I'll be right back." He smiled. "Going to run to the men's room."

Michael shared a mischievous look with Ellie and Olivia. "All right, we wait five minutes and then we follow."

"If we get caught…," Olivia worried.

"We won't get caught—trust me," Michael smiled.

"Our boy is being smart," Detective Adams remarked as he returned to the table. "Looks like he's deactivated one of the phones. We've only got a ping from one phone now."

"I'm sure he's got this all figured out," Michael replied.

"Here." Ellie handed him a bag with a hot croissant and a cup of coffee to go. "Got to keep you energized." She winked.

Detective Adams gave her a hug and then hugged Olivia. He turned to Michael and cocked an eyebrow. "I've got my eyes on you."

Michael tried to come up with something witty but all he could do was gulp.

Chapter 29

Chase

Michael backed a black Dodge Charger rental car into a parking spot behind Ned's Souvenir Shop, where they could keep an eye on the Bay Breeze Hotel. He pulled on a black baseball cap and affixed a Tom Selleck-approved mustache. A pair of Ray-Ban sunglasses completed the ensemble.

Ellie shook her head. "You look like a stripper."

"More like desperation," Olivia laughed.

"All right, guys, you know the plan. I'm going to hide out in the parking lot. As soon as I see him exit the hotel, I'll let you guys know."

"We know—Livs and I wait here till you get back."

"No, we're leaving without you," Olivia sighed.

Michael was about to reply when Ellie shoved him out the door.

"Go, go…you're wasting time."

Michael cut along behind a group of businesses, then crossed A1A. Traffic was light this time of morning. He jogged down a beach access ramp, then made his way along the beach to the hotel.

He crouched beside the hotel's seawall—the last thing he needed was Detective Adams's men to see him creeping around. Hopefully, they were all focused on Simon and the Bay Breeze. A six-foot chain-link fence separated him and the parking lot. Michael took one last glance at his surroundings and then deftly scaled the fence.

He crouched behind a red Toyota pickup truck and scanned the parking lot. All was quiet. A flock of seagulls played chase with the waves, rushing in as they receded, sprinting away as the waves tumbled back to the shore.

Michael threaded his way through the parking lot until he spotted Simon's yellow car. From his vantage point, he could see the front door of the hotel and his vehicle.

I'm in position, Michael texted.

Moments later, Ellie texted a thumbs-up.

Ten minutes passed. The sun was up and beating down on him. Sweat stung his eyes, and he was getting an incredibly bad headache from staring at the glass doors. *I should have brought some water.* Michael's legs were aching; he shifted from crouching to kneeling. He glanced at his watch. It was 6:30. Where was…?

Simon pushed the hotel door open, stepped outside, and then for a long moment, he studied the parking lot and surrounding area. He finally made his way to his car. Michael inched up just enough to see what Simon was doing.

He texted the girls: *He's at his car, heading over.*

Simon popped the trunk and threw his cell phone inside, then slammed it shut.

Michael hesitated as Simon walked away from his car and made his way deeper into the parking lot. He came to a stop in front of Whitney's car. He opened the backdoor and threw his luggage into the back seat.

Michael dashed to the back of the parking lot, racing along the rows of cars. Traffic was heavier now on A1A. He danced his way across the highway to the other side.

"He switched cars," he said excitedly as he slid into the driver's seat.

"What do you mean?" Ellie asked.

"He's driving Whitney's car." Michael edged the Dodge Charger around the souvenir shop, waiting for Simon to pull onto the highway. "He threw his phone into the yellow car's trunk," he explained. "He's betting if the police tried to find him by his phone, it will lead them to that car. He doesn't think they know about his burner phone."

Simon edged up to the highway in the burgundy Kia Optima. He turned right, heading north on A1A. A few seconds later, a silver Honda whipped out of the parking lot.

Michael pulled out behind the Honda. "The chase is on!"

Chapter 30

Rendezvous

Michael hung back, always keeping at least two cars between him and the undercover police car.

"You don't think he's leaving Lana Cove, do you?" Olivia asked, worried about jurisdiction.

Michael stole a glance at his watch. "I don't think so—he's only got eleven minutes to meet with his mystery man."

Simon turned left onto Auburn, past the library, and through Lana Cove's booming financial metropolis, consisting of a small, squat, brick building and a post office. Michael put even more distance between them, not wanting to spook Simon or the undercover cops.

Simon made another turn and pulled into the parking lot of a massive three-story structure that glistened in the sunlight as if the entire edifice was constructed of mirrors. A black sign with silver letters read "Glimmer Park Office Complex."

"Geez," Michael said, squinting. "Need a suntan? Just stand next to that building." The unmarked police car drove past the entrance. It would have been too obvious if they followed Simon into the office complex.

Michael pulled into Jasper's Boat Warehouse, parking across the street, while Olivia kept an eye on Simon.

"He's pulling around the back of the building," Olivia exclaimed. "We're going to lose him!"

The trio leaped from the car and dashed across the road into the parking lot. The glare from the building was intense. "I don't think they thought this through," Ellie said, shading her eyes with her hand.

"You guys stay behind me. He most likely won't recognize me." Two large glass doors swung open as they approached the entrance. A blast of air-conditioning met them as they stepped inside. Michael paused at a touchscreen directory. "There're dozens of companies here."

"Commercial office space," Ellie said. "Someone here is connected to Simon."

Across the lobby, a FedEx employee raised a steel gate with a rattle and flicked the lights on. Next door, the Starbucks sign flashed to life; another day of business was about to begin.

Olivia pointed to a set of glass doors on the other side of the building. "He parked around back. We need to hurry."

The trio walked quickly across the lobby. To their right, a series of stairs led to a carpeted area filled with benches, couches, and tables. Businesspeople were scattered throughout, conversing or hunched over their phones.

Michael nearly jumped out of his skin when the screech of a macaw echoed throughout the building. The magnificent parrot sat atop a golden perch, in the middle of a forest of ficus and bromeliads. An indoor stream, surrounded by rocks, trickled under a small bridge. "My heart," Michael moaned as he clutched his chest.

"His name is Merlot," Ellie laughed, reading a placard attached to his perch.

"I'm going to need a Merlot if he does that again," Michael declared.

They were just a few steps from the door when Olivia grabbed Michael's arm. "There he is!"

Michael and Ellie stopped in their tracks.

"Good job, Olivia,"

Simon sat on a wooden bench, reading a newspaper. He blended in perfectly with the other businessmen, dressed in loafers, beige khakis, and a light blue dress shirt. His rolling suitcase was festooned between his legs.

The trio backed away from the doorway to a window, where they could watch Simon without being seen. Michael glanced around the lobby. A line was beginning to form at the Starbucks. His stomach grumbled; he could go for a breakfast sandwich right now.

"Michael." Olivia nudged him. "Look."

A bespectacled elderly man, with a swirl of white hair atop his head, sat on the bench next to Simon. He took a long drag from his cigarette and then flicked it across the courtyard.

"Don't tell me that grandpa is his secret contact." Michael had a look of dismay on his face. "The guy's like ninety. He may die before Simon makes the drop."

Ellie and Olivia nodded. If this wasn't the guy, then whoever he was supposed to meet with was late.

The old man picked up Simon's newspaper. From their vantage point, they could see him slip something inside. He placed the newspaper back on the bench between them.

"Obviously a speed reader," Michael whispered.

Simon looked around the courtyard. Seeming satisfied, he unsnapped his small travel bag, reached inside, and sat a thermos on the bench between them.

He folded the newspaper, put it under his arm, stood, and was about to walk away when Detective Adams and two plainclothes officers arrived.

The old man stood shakily, clutching the thermos to his chest. And then with blinding speed, he lashed out with the thermos and struck an officer in the head. Before he could react, he kicked out viciously, toppling the other officer. Without a backward glance, he hurdled the bench and raced into the lobby.

Michael dove for the man but missed. He slid across the floor, making an unsettling squeaky flesh sound. The old man sprinted through the lobby and up a flight of stairs, disappearing down a hallway.

"You're out!" someone yelled from the lounge area.

"Ouch," Michael groaned as he climbed slowly to his feet. His mustache remained glued to the floor, a sad reminder of his failed attempt.

Two undercover police officers raced inside. "That way," Michael groaned, pointing to the stairs.

Chapter 31

Invisible

Michael joined Olivia and Ellie back at the window. "What I wouldn't give to know what he's saying to Simon," Olivia whispered.

Detective Adams's face was inches from Simon's. He snatched the newspaper from him and shook it in his face. It was at that moment that Simon saw his opportunity. He slipped his burner phone from his pocket and dropped it behind his rolling luggage. Then with a well-placed snap of his foot, he kicked it backward into a drain.

"His phone," Michael gasped. "He just kicked his phone." He was about to dash outside when Olivia grabbed him by the arm.

"Michael, if my uncle sees us—"

"I'll be right back," Michael said as he raced away across the lobby.

Detective Adams spun Simon around and handcuffed him. The other officer carefully searched through his luggage, and then gave the nod that it was okay to transport. Detective Adams reached into his pants pocket and retrieved his cell phone. He shook his head and jabbed Simon in the chest, who smiled and shrugged his shoulders.

No one paid any attention to the tanned UPS driver dressed in brown shorts and a brown top, his hair graying at his temples. He carried a small stack of boxes down the stairs, winked at Olivia and Ellie, then made his way out the front door, to his brown van, and drove away.

Chapter 32

Cornered

Simon sat in the interrogation room, a cocky smile on his face.

"Where's your phone?" Detective Adams demanded.

"I told you, that crazy old man that beat up your men took it. Are you going to charge me with a crime? Because as far as I know, having an airline ticket isn't illegal in this country."

Detective Adams pushed back from the table and pounded his fist on it, a vein pulsing in his forehead.

Simon looked up at him coolly. "Is that supposed to intimidate me? You have zero evidence. What you do have is pure conjecture. So, before I have my lawyer ream your captain out, I want to know: Am I being charged or not? That's the way they do it right? I mean on all the cop shows on television that's the way it works."

Detective Adams leaned forward, trembling with anger. "You're free to go for now, but you're not to leave Lana Cove. Understand?" He walked out of the interrogation room and slammed the door. He turned to Officer Lark. "Process him. He's free to go."

"Wait!" yelled Olivia, bursting into the precinct with Michael and Ellie on her heels, just as Simon was being led out of the interrogation room.

"Olivia, now's not the time...," Detective Adams said, an edge to his voice.

"We have something for you." She handed him a plastic bag with a small black phone inside.

Detective Adams's eyes traveled from Olivia to Michael. "What happened to you?"

Michael shook his head. "Honestly, you don't want to know."

Simon's face paled. "What's the matter?" Michael smiled. "You should be happy; we found your phone. It's such a pain getting back all those memories—"

"That's not my phone, you idiot," Simon hissed. "My phone's at the hotel—I forgot it this morning."

"I know," Michael smiled, "in the trunk of your rental. But that's a story for another day."

Detective Adams looked from Michael back to Simon, back to Michael.

"This is Simon's burner phone," Olivia smiled. "I think you'll find it incredibly valuable to your investigation."

"That's not my phone!" Simon screamed.

"Then you'll see the irony," Michael said, "when the GPS data aligns perfectly with your every movement—and let's not forget about those pesky little fingerprints they'll be able to recover—"

"Thank you, Michael. I believe we can handle it from here," Detective Adams interrupted.

"But, I was just getting started…."

Detective Adams smiled at Simon and pointed to the interrogation room. "Shall we?"

Detective Mitchell, a thin athletic man with thick black hair, graying at the temples joined Olivia, Michael, and Ellie outside a two-way window that allowed them to see and hear Detective Adams. A young woman with short blonde hair sat at the table beside him. Simon's phone was attached to a laptop, and on her screen, a satellite view of the GPS data.

"Why can't *you* do that?" Olivia said, punching Michael's shoulder.

"That's Cheryl Miller," Detective Mitchell explained. "Graduated at the top of her class in computer science at NCU. She's a digital assassin," he said, shaking his head.

"Here's a timeline," Cheryl said, a slight southern drawl to her voice. She turned her laptop so Detective Adams could see.

Simon sat quietly. A line of perspiration glistened on his forehead, his bravado nowhere to be found.

"Oak Green Cemetery at one in the morning. What were you doing there, Simon?" Detective Adams asked.

Simon remained silent as Cheryl's fingers tapped the keyboard. "He traveled from the cemetery to the Bay Breeze Hotel."

"What about this address?"

Cheryl looked at Detective Adams's notes, nodded, and a few moments later turned the laptop back again so he could see the screen.

"Simon, why were you at Peyton Leek's house?"

Simon remained silent.

"Let's see if we can put two and two together. I think that you and Whitney killed Hugo. I'm guessing we'll find his body at the cemetery, and I bet you killed Peyton to keep his mouth shut." He leaned in toward Simon. "It's only a matter of time before we know everything."

"Look," Simon spat, "I didn't kill Hugo. He was my friend." Simon's face twisted angrily. "That lying, conniving girlfriend of his killed him. She never liked me and set me up."

Detective Adams let his face soften and nodded his head, encouraging Simon to keep talking.

"Why would I kill Hugo?" Simon's eyes looked to a place above Detective Adams's head. "I had a little thing going on the side. Collectors would pay good money for rare artifacts." He shook his head. "A pharaoh's ring, a solid gold statue of his cat with jeweled eyes—"

Simon was silent for a moment. He stared at his hands, opening and closing them slowly.

"Everyone does it. Everyone. The man that I met today paid me $250,000 a couple weeks ago and transferred another 250 to my account. It's easy money. The customs officials are easily bribed...."

"Simon." Detective Adams spoke softly. "Why did you go to Peyton's house?"

"To give him more money. He caught me removing the seals and retrieving the artifacts from the sarcophagus. I didn't realize the isolation unit had cameras. I paid him $5,000 to keep his mouth shut, and to destroy the video—

"He cornered me at the museum and said that the police were asking him a lot of questions, so I agreed to bring him another $5,000, only he wouldn't answer the door. I figured he'd changed his mind."

"I see." Detective Adams nodded. "What about the graveyard? Why does your phone put you at the graveyard?"

Simon exhaled. "It's where I met my contact for the first time. He wanted me to watch while he wired $250,000 into my Caiman account. He wanted to show me how easy it would be to do business with him. Let me tell you, there's something about seeing a number followed by all those zeroes magically appear in your account."

"Who is your contact?"

"I don't know. But he had insider information on the expedition. I figured he was working with one of the locals."

"How did he find you?"

"As I said, there is a sophisticated network of smuggling from Egypt. I received an email with very specific instructions. The man knew exactly what he wanted and the value of each. I was told to secure those items and send proof when they were through customs. He told me he would pay me half a million dollars. It was a no-brainer."

"So those are the images on your phone?"

"Yes."

A light tap on the door brought Detective Adams to his feet. Detective Mitchell poked his head in the door. "Sorry, Louie, but I've got Alex Ross on the phone from Oak Green Cemetery. He's ready for us."

Detective Adams turned and leaned on the table. "Thank you for opening up," he told Simon. "We'll finish up when I return."

Chapter 33

Oak Green Cemetery

Michael, Ellie, and Olivia sat in the car while Detective Adams spoke with the director of the Oak Green Cemetery. He was a pale, thin man, his white cheeks mottled with rosacea. He wore his thinning red hair in a hard part. His forest green suit was the same color as the peeling logo on the wrought iron gates at the cemetery's entrance. His tie was a tired, faded gold that had given up its vibrancy dozens of dry cleanings ago.

There was a lot of nodding going on, which Michael interpreted as progress. A handshake between the two men signaled they had reached an agreement.

Detective Adams walked to his black SUV and motioned for them to follow him. The cars followed a serpentine paved road that coiled like a snake amongst gravestones. Dark clouds rolled like tumbleweeds across the sky, threatening rain.

Michael shifted in his seat, letting his mind wander. *Would we find Hugo's body?* It seemed hard to believe that someone larger than life could be dead.

Ellie and Olivia were quiet as well, each absorbed by their own thoughts. Death did that to people...made them reflect on their own mortality. The SUV's brake lights flashed. The word *stop* penetrated Michael's thoughts. He shifted the car into park and cut the engine.

Detective Adams and Officer Lewis, a square-jawed, broad-shouldered transplant from Texas, climbed out of the SUV and made their way over to a freshly dug grave.

"I guess that's our cue," Michael said quietly.

Ellie and Olivia nodded solemnly.

A gray sedan pulled up behind their car, followed by a white CSU van and a Lana Cove squad car. Everyone exited their vehicles and congregated in front of the grave.

Detective Adams turned a wary eye to the sky, then turned his attention to the group. "Afternoon, everyone. This is Alex Ross—he's the director of Oak Green Cemetery."

Alex nodded to the crowd gathered around him. "Good afternoon, everyone."

"Good morning," the crowd said, echoing his greeting.

"According to Mr. Ross, the gentleman buried here is Fred Myers. He's a widower, without any immediate family. Our job is to be thorough yet respectful, understood?"

Everyone responded affirmatively in unison.

An orange backhoe made its way up the road toward them. A specialized bucket attachment for digging graves was connected to its rear by a large arm resembling the tail of a scorpion. A workman dressed in drab green clothes, work boots, and a green hat trudged along behind the backhoe. A shovel and pickaxe jostled on his shoulder.

"John will clear away the dirt," Alex explained, "and then we'll raise the coffin. The dirt is still soft, so it won't take long."

"This is an awkward question." Michael made an embarrassed face. "But, before the coffin is lowered, do they...check the grave?"

Alex smiled. "Not an awkward question at all. We don't thoroughly examine the grave per se, but yes, we do make sure the grave is completely empty before placing the coffin."

"Thank you."

John pulled up alongside the grave and stopped. He climbed down out of the backhoe's cabin and jumped to the ground. He was a short man, with gray, bristly hair. His lined face revealed that he had not lived an easy life. Michael detected a slight limp as the man made his way to the cluster of people gathered around the gravesite.

"Everyone, this is John. He'll be operating the backhoe. And that's Carl. He's John's assistant."

Carl nodded and mouthed, "Afternoon."

"John, this is Detective Adams. He's in charge of the investigation."

"Afternoon, sir," John said, shaking his hand. His voice was quiet, calming. "It's going to take about ten minutes to reach the coffin, and then another ten to get the harness connected. So, plan on about twenty minutes."

"Thank you, John." Detective Adams nodded. He turned to the two uniformed officers who had arrived in the squad car. "Rogers, Morris, I need you to establish a perimeter. We need to keep the lookie-loos away."

"Yes, sir," they replied and hurried away.

The backhoe's engine rumbled to life. Under John's skilled hands, the backhoe made quick work of the soft dirt. Less than ten minutes had passed, and there was already a mountain of dirt.

Carl held up his gloved hand, signaling for him to stop. He removed his hat, revealing long, sweaty hair, and wiped his forehead with his sleeve. He tossed his shovel into the grave, then climbed inside.

John hopped down from the backhoe, grabbed a tangled series of cables with hooks and straps, and then stood patiently waiting as the other gravedigger cleared away the rest of the dirt from the coffin.

"Good enough," Carl called out. "I'm ready for the harness." He grabbed the harness from John and worked the cables through the handles that surrounded the coffin. John climbed back into the backhoe and maneuvered the bucket directly over the grave. Together, he and Carl attached the cable. Moments later, the casket was free from the grave.

A hush fell over the crowd as reality settled in.

Ellie dropped her head to her chest. "If you guys don't mind, I think I'll wait in the car. I'd prefer to remember Hugo the way he was."

Olivia gave her a gentle hug. "I think I'll join you."

John maneuvered away from the grave, turned the backhoe, and slowly lowered the casket. A CSU agent, dressed in a white jumpsuit and blue latex gloves, climbed into the grave.

Detective Adams, Alex Ross, and the crime scene photographer circled the rectangular hole. It was only a matter of minutes when the CSU officer looked up. "Sir, we have a body."

Michael exhaled. He knew they were going to find Hugo's body, but nothing could prepare him for those words.

Chapter 34

Unexpected

"Michael." Ellie's voice wavered. "Louie said that Hugo's body was wrapped in black plastic."

"Yes," Michael nodded, "just like the piece of plastic that we found. I gave it to Detective Adams at the crime scene. He wasn't too happy with me, but it certainly ties everything together for him."

"Okay, that's what I wanted to check on."

Michael pulled into the guest parking area of the police station. The sun had lost its battle, and now big splotchy drops of rain began to fall. The smell of wet asphalt was strong as they dashed to the doorway of the police precinct.

"So," Olivia said as they stepped inside, "Whitney and Simon were in this together. I can't believe it."

"It looks that way," Michael conceded. He'd been excited about solving the case, but this wasn't the ending he had expected.

"I helped her. I even felt sorry for her," Olivia said angrily. "Hugo was a jerk, but he didn't deserve to die."

Ellie walked in silence beside them, her arms across her chest, feeling like she was in a dream. If only she could wake up, this would all be over.

Detective Mitchell greeted them as they made their way to Detective Adams's office. "Louie filled me in on everything. Horrible stuff," he said, making a face. "I've sent for Whitney. She'll be in interrogation room two; Simon will be in room one."

"Thank you," Olivia said. "We'll wait by the observation window."

A uniformed officer appeared with three bottles of water. "You guys look like you could use this." He smiled as he passed them out.

Detective Adams stopped by the observation room. He gave Olivia and Ellie a hug. "Hopefully we'll get to the bottom of this. I'm going to interrogate Simon while Mitchell speaks to Whitney."

"Thanks, Louie," Ellie said. "It will be good to finally find out the truth."

Simon looked anxiously at Detective Adams, who sat in front of him, methodically reading through his notes. He leaned forward, staring into Simon's eyes, looking for the smallest telltale reaction when he said the words, "We found Hugo's body."

To his credit, Simon sat perfectly still, his eyes glued on Detective Adams. He breathed calmly through his nose.

Detective Adams slid a picture over to Simon.

Simon slowly lowered his gaze to the photo. He closed his eyes for a moment, grabbed the photo, and flipped it over.

"The gig's up, Simon." He placed a clear, plastic evidence baggy on the table.

Simon looked at the bag, confused. "I'm not sure I understand what this is."

"This is a piece of plastic that was found on the locking mechanism of your rental car. How much do you want to bet that forensics is going to find a matching tear on the bag identical to the one we found Hugo's body in? Do you think that forensics is going to determine that this piece of plastic we found in your car came from the same bag?"

"It was Whitney!" Simon shouted. "I can't take the blame for this, and I won't. She got into a huge fight with Hugo. She was tired of his infidelity, sleeping around with anybody and everybody. He used her, made her feel like a fool. On top of that, he was about to replace her. He'd just hired another twenty-two-year-old intern, fresh out of college.... Whitney could see the writing on the wall."

Simon looked down and shook his head. "She told Hugo she was going to put an end to all of his cheating... I didn't know that she was going to kill him."

"Then what happened," Detective Adams prompted, "after you heard them arguing?"

"I thought for sure that security was going to come, but then the yelling stopped. I figured they had finally gone to sleep."

"What time was this?"

"About midnight, I think. I'm not sure—I just know it was late. I'd just fallen asleep when I heard a knock at my door. Whitney was trembling and crying. She said something terrible had happened."

Detective Adams flicked his hand for him to continue.

"She said she'd given Hugo a little something to knock him out, but he'd had some kind of allergic reaction...." Simon's voice softened. "That he had died."

"So, you put Hugo in the trunk of your car?"

"Yes, we manhandled him down the stairwell. I backed my car up to the back of the hotel and we put him in my trunk. We didn't know what to do; we just panicked. Then I remembered my meeting at the graveyard and seeing a freshly dug grave. So, we broke in and buried his body. The workers had left a couple shovels, so we used those to dig the grave a little deeper and covered him with dirt.

"We came up with the idea of saying that he never came back to the hotel. She thought it was the perfect touch filing that missing person's report."

Simon lowered his head. Tears fell from his eyes, splashing on the table. His voice caught in his throat. "I should have just come in. It was an accident; she didn't mean to kill him. But she was so scared, and she threatened to come to the police about me smuggling goods into the country if I didn't help."

Simon's hands shook uncontrollably. Tears poured down his face. "Hugo was a monster. He didn't know when to quit womanizing, and he didn't care how many people he hurt. I know what I did was wrong—but it wasn't Whitney's fault either. It was just an accident. She couldn't have known that whatever she gave him would kill him. She's a good person...she's just scared."

Simon sobbed and lowered his forehead to the table. "Now both of our lives are destroyed. Why, why did this have to happen?"

"She didn't kill him," said a voice with absolute certainty.

Michael, Ellie, and Olivia whirled around, surprised to hear Ivan's voice behind them.

"Ivan?" Michael exclaimed.

"In the flesh." He smiled. "Except my real name is Milo."

"That's right," Michael exclaimed. "What are you doing here?" The others stared in shock.

"I'm here to help you catch a killer." He shook a large envelope. "The real killer," he said, raising his eyebrows.

Detective Mitchell smiled. "Ivan's been a busy man. It's time for some fireworks."

Chapter 35

Exposed

Detective Adams spun in his chair, angry at being disturbed, especially when a perp was confessing to accessory after the fact.

"Detective, I need to interrupt you for just a moment."

"Mitchell, I'm right in the middle of an—"

"Louie, trust me."

Simon's eyes grew wide when Milo followed Detective Adams into the interrogation room. "What's he doing here?" he hissed.

"Ivan's been quite busy. I've been told that he's got quite an eye for photography. Milo, if you would."

Milo shook a stack of photos from the envelope onto the steel table. "This first picture…," Ivan slid it so Simon could see, "…was taken the night of Hugo's disappearance. That's you, placing something huge into the trunk of your car. I thought you were stealing a mummy or something valuable from the museum," Ivan said. "I didn't think you had the stones to kill a man."

Simon sat silently staring, the color drained from his face.

"And here you are...," Ivan slid another photo over, "...handing a *lot* of cash to a mechanic at the car rental place. And another at the florist. I thought that you were buying flowers for Hugo's grave. But Detective Mitchell tells me those flowers are called monkshood and are extremely poisonous. Should I continue, Detective?" Milo asked.

"Yes, please. I'm quite enjoying this."

"And then I heard on the news that a man named Peyton Leek, the night guard at the museum, was found dead in his home. And look who turned up at his house? Here's Peyton opening the front door for you, and then here's you leaving about thirty minutes later."

"I've got more." Ivan smiled wickedly at Simon. "But I see the cat's got your tongue."

"I thought you hated Hugo," Simon growled. "You said you were going to destroy him."

"Oh that. Hugo was setting a trap for you. Seems like you've made a livelihood of stealing relics and artifacts. The Egyptian government had approached Hugo about restricting his access to dig sites, etc., until he put an end to the thefts. That's where I, Milo

Kaminski, award-winning investigative journalist, came in."

Simon's mouth dropped open. "You were working with Hugo?"

"For months." Milo nodded. "He hired me to monitor your activities. He wanted to prove beyond a doubt that it was *you* that was behind the thefts."

"You're an idiot. Whitney killed Hugo—the proof was in her room."

"Give it up, Simon. While you were killing Hugo, Whitney was sitting in front of Ellie's house crying. She was sure Ellie and Hugo were—"

"Detective Adams." Simon turned his attention from Milo. "I can prove that Whitney was at the graveyard. Check her phone."

"We did. And yes, there was a trip to the graveyard in her GPS data. However, she claims that the night that Hugo disappeared, you came into her room to check on her. After you left, Whitney tried to check her phone, but it was missing. She said that you returned a couple hours later under the pretense of looking for Hugo and that you had mistakenly picked up her phone.

"The timestamps on her keycard and the dozen or so calls from her room proved that she wasn't at the graveyard, and I'm sure as soon as I pull the traffic-cam footage—" Detective Adams's words hung in the air.

A scowl formed on Simon's face. "Everyone loved Hugo," he exclaimed bitterly. "All of his exciting stories and that freakishly large smile. He'd never stop smiling. I hated him—every single fiber of the man's being disgusted me. Yes, I killed Hugo and I would do it again and again. Only next time, I wouldn't get caught."

Ellie, Michael, and Olivia reeled back, shocked by Simon's confession.

"Finally," Ellie whispered. "It's finally over."

Chapter 36

A Gift

"I noticed you're walking a little better today," Detective Adams said nonchalantly to Michael.

"Yeah, that was one tough game of beach volleyball. Still getting the sand out of my shorts."

"Must have been brutal. I mean, with all those scrapes on your hands and wrists."

"You should have seen the other guy—guys—guys' team," Michael clarified.

"Who was surprised when Milo showed up unexpectantly?" Olivia asked, giving Michael a much-needed reprieve from questioning.

"I never expected to see him again, not in a million years," Ellie agreed.

"Oh, Uncle Louie, I have one more question. What happened to the old man? You know, Simon's mystery accomplice."

Detective Adams took a sip of coffee. Michael thought he looked a little uncomfortable answering the question. "Well, it turns out he wasn't an old man at all. We found an exceptionally lifelike mask and his clothes in a bathroom stall upstairs."

"Well, that explains a thing or two." Oliva nodded.

"Any idea as to what's going to happen to the expedition? To Hugo's legacy?" asked Michael.

"I think I know the answer to that question," a familiar voice answered.

"Whitney!" Ellie cried, jumping to her feet. She rushed around the table, throwing her arms around her. Olivia joined in.

Michael arched an eyebrow at Detective Adams. "I noticed you don't embrace me that way."

"Try it and I'll snap you like a twig," he replied, cocking an eyebrow.

"I just wanted to stop by and thank you all. Especially you, Michael. I know that you went above and beyond—especially after how I treated you." Whitney shook her head, "Hugo was wrong about you—you *are* an adventurer."

"Thank you, Whitney," Michael said kindly. "So, what's next for you?"

"I'm going to honor Hugo's contract with the museums on this tour, and after that, I'm going back to school. I've always wanted to be a teacher."

"You're going to make a great teacher." Michael stood. "May I?"

Whitney rushed to him, giving him a huge hug. "You know," she said, stepping back and giving him a mischievous smile. "You're not too bad for an old guy."

Olivia playfully bumped shoulders with Ellie. "Looks like someone is moving in on your territory," she whispered.

Ellie rolled her eyes. "We gotta let them win occasionally."

Whitney turned to Detective Adams. He stood and held out his hand. She took in a deep breath, brushed his hand aside, and leaned in and gave him a hug. "Thank you for seeing this through. You're a good man. Scary...but good." She grinned.

"I'll take that." Detective Adams laughed, his cheeks red with embarrassment.

"All right, everyone, I'm off," Whitney announced. "If you're ever in New York—"

"Definitely." Ellie beamed.

The four friends sat in silence for a moment. It seemed like only yesterday when Whitney had walked through that door with Hugo for the first time.

"Well...," Ellie stood, finally breaking the silence, "Livs and I have got a lot of work to catch up on and a stack of bills to pay."

"About that...," started Michael.

"You want a job?" Olivia exclaimed.

"Ahem." Michael cleared his throat. "As you well know, I already *have* a job. I'm a—"

"Unemployed bum," Detective Adams offered.

"I was going to say writer. I'm sure everyone remembers the case that we helped the Lana Cove police crack. You know which one I'm talking about, Louie."

Detective Adams furrowed his brow and growled at Michael.

"Okay, I get it," Michael said, holding up his hands. "Not yet, not yet. In that exciting case, we helped recover a few stolen items that may or may not have been worth a few million dollars."

"Oh my God, Michael, get on with it!" Olivia shook the table.

Michael pulled out his wallet and slid a check across the table to Ellie and Olivia.

"Seventeen thousand dollars?! Michael," Ellie gasped.

Olivia stared at the check, shocked. "This better not be a joke."

"Nope, it's not a joke. The Centennial Insurance Company sent me a check for $50,000 for returning the paintings and the stamp. I figured it was only fair that we split the reward money three ways."

Ellie and Olivia jumped to their feet, sandwiching Michael in a hug.

"Thank you so much, Michael. You don't know how badly we needed this. This is honestly—"

"A lifesaver." Olivia laughed.

Ellie leaned in and kissed Michael on the cheek. "You've earned a day off." She winked.

Michael's heart was filled with joy and love for his friends—but there was one other emotion he had not expected, and that was pride; he finally saw a hint of acceptance, of friendship, in a simple head nod and wink from Detective Louie Adams.

More from T. Lockhaven

We hope you enjoyed reading *A Mummy to Die For*, the second book in *The Coffee House Sleuths* series. Let us know what you think by leaving a review on Amazon, Barnes & Noble and/or Goodreads. Thank you so very much!

The Coffee House Sleuths (Ongoing Series)

Book 1: A Garden to Die For
Book 2: A Mummy to Die For
Book 3: A Role to Die For (Upcoming)

Also written in the series is *Sleighed*, the first book in *The Coffee House Sleuths: A Christmas Cozy Mystery*. *Sleighed* takes place in the same town, with the same characters, but was written as a fun standalone Christmas story.

T. Lockhaven is also a children's author under the name Thomas Lockhaven.

Ava & Carol Detective Agency (Ongoing Series)

Book 1: The Mystery of the Pharaoh's Diamonds
Book 2: The Mystery of Solomon's Ring
Book 3: The Haunted Mansion
Book 4: Dognapped
Book 5: The Eye of God
Book 6: The Crown Jewels Mystery
Book 7: The Curse of the Red Devil

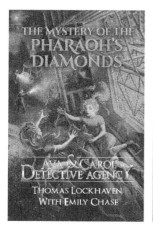  

DOGNAPPED

AVA & CAROL DETECTIVE AGENCY

THOMAS LOCKHAVEN
WITH EMILY CHASE

THE EYE OF GOD

AVA & CAROL DETECTIVE AGENCY

THOMAS LOCKHAVEN

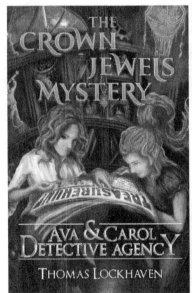

THE CROWN JEWELS MYSTERY

AVA & CAROL DETECTIVE AGENCY

THOMAS LOCKHAVEN

THE CURSE OF THE RED DEVIL

AVA & CAROL DETECTIVE AGENCY

THOMAS LOCKHAVEN
WITH EMILY CHASE

Quest Chasers (Ongoing Series)

Book 1: The Deadly Cavern
Book 2: The Screaming Mummy

The Ghosts of Ian Stanley (Ongoing Series)

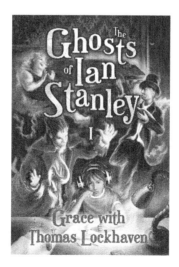

Book Releases

Learn about new book releases by following T. Lockhaven's author page on Amazon or on Bookbub. You may also sign up for our newsletter at the following website: twistedkeypublishing.com

Made in the USA
Monee, IL
07 July 2023

38650538R00142